Poker Chips and Poison

A Silvermoon Retirement Village Mystery

Poker Chips and Poison

A Silvermoon
Retirement Village
Mystery

RODNEY STRONG

Published by LoreQuinn Publishing

This is a work of fiction. Names, characters, places, and incidents either are the production of the author's imagination or are used fictitiously, and any resemblance to actual persons, living or dead, events, or locales is entirely coincidental.

Editor: Anna Golden

Front cover design: www.stunningbookcovers.com

Printing by: YourBooks

A catalogue record for this book is available from the National Library of New Zealand.

Also by Rodney Strong

Hitchhiker books
Murder in Paint
Murder in Mud
Murder in Doubt

Standalone books
Troy's Possibilities

For children
Written as R.G Strong
Karmartha, The Last Garden
Escape from School

ONƐ

Alice eyed her opponent. The next ten seconds were crucial. The next ten seconds meant the difference between ongoing torment or a swift end. It all came down to one thing:

Was that a poker face, or was she dead?

Alice had to admit, around here some days it was hard to tell.

Time was running out. She had to make a move.

With a confidence she didn't feel she looked at her hand, then lay the cards on the table.

'Flush.'

All eyes went to the woman sitting opposite Alice. The collective breaths of all four at the table stopped — a dangerous situation at the Silvermoon Retirement Village.

Teresa threw her cards down in disgust. 'All I had was a pair of tens.'

The others at the table laughed as Alice dragged the pile of chips towards her.

'Why on earth did you go all in on a pair of tens? I had more than that and I folded,' Owen said. A tall, solid man in his early eighties, he still dressed as if he was going into the office. White shirt, short-sleeved in summer, long-sleeved in winter (but never with the arms rolled up), a dark tie which could be anything from burgundy to deep blue (but nothing gauche like yellow or heaven forbid with pictures on it), and slacks.

'I thought she was bluffing. I was sure of it,' Teresa protested.

'And why were you so sure?' Betty asked in her soft Irish accent. Despite living in New Zealand for more than forty years, it was still there and became more prominent when she was accusing someone of something. Betty was short and leathery, a lifetime of working outside on a farm had dried and darkened her skin. Alice suspected that she and Owen were involved. If Alice had had anything more than a casual desire to know she could have found out in no time, but she figured everyone here had earned the right to some privacy just by making it this far in life.

'Well, she...' Teresa trailed off.

'Rubbed my earlobe?' Alice finished. She smiled at Teresa's open mouthed response. 'It's only a tell if you don't know you're doing it.' She winked and the table laughed again.

'I'll have to pay you when I get to the bank,' Teresa said with a scowl.

'None of that. 'That's what internet banking is for.'

'I hardly think internet banking was set up to pay poker debts,' Teresa snapped at Owen, her fluffy brown hair bouncing as she shook her head.

It was always the same with her, Alice thought. Teresa always demanded her winnings straight away. However if she lost, which she more often did, there was some excuse about not having money on her, or being a little short until pension day. Given how much it cost to live in this place, no one believed she had to wait for her government pension to pay her debts.

Faced with stern expressions from her friends, Teresa adjusted her glasses, then meekly lifted her phone off the table, tapped on the screen, and a few seconds later Alice heard her own phone ping. It wasn't the first time she'd won money from those at the table. She might not know what a google was, but Alice made sure, with the help of her granddaughter, that she knew how to send money (and more importantly how to receive money) from her circle of friends.

She made sure to lose occasionally. Not that she was a card shark, but she had spent most of her working life reading people, and found it came in useful on occasion, even in a sedate place like the retirement village.

'I'm afraid I must go. This new woman is going to teach us how to make cats out of clay shortly,' Betty said.

Alice blinked. She could think of worse ways to spend the afternoon, but not many.

As her friends left the room, for a moment Alice had the shared space to herself. She looked out the large window that overlooked the back garden. The retirement complex sat on an acre of prime land on one of the many tree covered hills surrounding Wellington city. It was tucked away amongst all the suburban houses and many people didn't know the extent of the village that was at the end of the long driveway. A short trip down the hill would have taken her to a city filled with countless cafes and designer shops, but Alice didn't drive and had no great urgency for either coffee or clothes. When she was younger and had more energy it had been different. The population had been lower, and no one on the street had had their heads buried in their phones because phones were usually attached to kitchen walls. Or maybe what had changed was how she viewed them. Back then everyone, man or woman, was a potential target. Now that she was retired, her perception had changed. Mostly.

She sneezed. The simple act caused a different response now that she was approaching the century mark. She would never have guessed that a sneeze could cause her ribs to hurt, or a twinge to appear in her back, or occasionally make her pee. Somehow the fact she had almost no body padding left made it worse. Standing, she stretched one way, then the other and her muscles eased.

Alice considered sitting back down but there were several residents she preferred not to run into, especially Gordon, who considered himself God's gift to women over seventy. He was a bit handsy and at their last encounter she had only just resisted the temptation to put one of those hands in a cast. Breaking bones, unlike so many other things was more about angles and leverage than strength.

Following the plush carpeted hallway, brightly lit by sunshine through a skylight, Alice entered the waiting elevator and pushed the button for the second floor. From this side of the main building you could get to any level. From reception though, visitors needed to be buzzed in by a staff member. It wasn't so much an issue of security as it was the discretion that money bought.

Exiting into a small landing she punched her code into the panel next to the door on the left, one of only two on the floor.

Her apartment would have rivalled the poshest hotel. The open plan living area and kitchen was filled with modern comfortable furniture, and her floor-to-ceiling windows overlooked the perfectly manicured front lawn and driveway. To the left, past the kitchen, was a guest bathroom, and through a door at the opposite end of the lounge was the bedroom, complete with ensuite and walk in wardrobe, which Alice privately thought was a step too far. She routinely wore two outfits, one was on and the other in the wash, and had a third pair of pants and blouse for best. The rest was empty space.

The bathroom was another matter. She spent much longer in the tiled, walk in shower than she needed to get clean, because the multiple jets hit spots she couldn't anymore. Sometimes she considered carrying a chair in there and drifting off to sleep. After all, if her skin turned prune-like not many people would notice the difference.

Alice turned on the television, flicked through some channels, then turned it off again. Even with the movie channel available to all residents and playing the latest pictures from around the world, there was nothing that caught her fancy enough to sit through.

She thought about making a snack, or better yet, having one sent up from the restaurant kitchen. Glancing at the clock she decided against it. Brunch was never a meal she'd warmed to. That's what snacks were for, to bridge the gap between breakfast and lunch. No need to create new meals just for the sake of it.

Alice eased her wiry frame out of the chair and walked around the couch. It wasn't until the third rotation that she admitted to herself what was bugging her.

She blamed Oliver. Although technically she could blame her granddaughter Amanda for introducing Oliver to her. Or she could blame Violet Tumbleton, her long dead friend, for not staying dead. But Violet was gone again, Amanda away working, so Oliver squarely took the blame.

She thought she had been content pottering around, her previous life a fond memory, until Oliver Atkinson showed up at her door asking for help to solve a murder. Alice should have said no. He wasn't a detective, amateur or otherwise. He was a writer (and not a bad one judging by the books she had read), a father of two under-ten-year-olds, one of which showed great promise in a life of manipulation, and a husband to an incredibly patient wife. But a detective he was not, which was probably why he had asked for her help.

Yes, she probably should have said no. But she hadn't, because maybe she wasn't as content as she'd thought. And they had caught the murderer, which she'd found quite exhilarating. Now, at the age of 97, winning money from her friends at poker was no longer very satisfying.

With a sigh Alice sat back down in front of the television and randomly picked a movie. The leading man was handsome, but couldn't act to save himself (and had probably never had to).

TWO

The bright sunshine flooding through the windows did little to dispel her melancholy the next morning. Not needing as much sleep as she used to, Alice was up and dressed by 6:30. She cooked herself a poached egg on toast, took the many pills that her doctor had prescribed and that she grudgingly took, and was flicking through the morning paper that was delivered to her front door six mornings a week.

The murder case had made the front page, and there was a quote from Detective Wilson acknowledging the public for providing vital information which led to the arrest.

Alice snorted, "providing vital information" indeed. She and Oliver had solved the whole damn thing for them. All the police had had to do was show up and slap on the handcuffs.

Alice turned to the crossword, picked up a pen and worked her way through from top to bottom. She was just working out a seven letter bird that started with B and ended in G when there was a knock at her door. Visitors were few, and those that did come were usually residents or staff of the village. There were a few of both she would be happy to avoid talking to.

She retrieved her phone from the coffee table and opened an app to a live stream video of the hallway beyond her front door. It wasn't something the management were aware of. Amanda had installed it for Alice when she first moved in. It made both of them feel better knowing she could check the door before opening it.

Owen stood in the hallway, shuffling back and forth on the spot. Alice put down her phone and went to usher her friend inside.

'Sorry to call around so early,' he said, once he was perched on a kitchen stool with a piping hot cup of herbal tea in front of him.

Alice thought he looked tired. And distracted. His top button was undone, a casual oversight to anyone else, but a concern to her.

She let him sip his drink and order his thoughts. Owen had been the chief executive of a bank before he'd retired a decade ago. She knew he liked to compose himself and consider all angles before making a decision. Most of the time it was an endearing quality, except for when they were playing poker. His tell was that he took longer than normal to decide on a bet when he was bluffing. Weighing risks versus rewards had been ingrained in him by a lifetime of management.

'Bunting,' she finally said to break the silence.

'Excuse me?' he said with wide eyes.

'Seven letter bird starting with B and ending with G. A bunting. It was in this morning's crossword.'

'Ah. I never had the time to do the crossword while I was working, and it's a bit late to take it up now.' He grinned briefly and she caught a glimpse of the handsome man he had been, before time and stress wore him out. The smile fell away and he looked troubled once more.

'Is it Betty?' she guessed.

He looked surprised. 'Is what Betty?'

'Whatever's on your mind.'

He hesitated, sucking on his teeth in a manner Alice found irritating.

'The thing is, I don't know if it's even a thing. Or if it is, whether it's a big thing or a small thing or nothing at all. Do you see?'

'Not the foggiest.'

He laughed. 'No, I'm doing a terrible job at explaining it. You see, it's this—' He broke off to cough, a chest-rattling sound that echoed off the walls, and took longer than Alice liked to get under control. She had endured a similar cough recently. Colds definitely went in the cons column of growing old.

Owen cleared his throat. 'Sorry, some tea must have gone down the wrong way.'

'I never understood that saying,' Alice replied. 'There's only one way down and one way up.'

'Very true. It goes on the long list of strange sayings that don't make sense,' Owen said.

'Speaking of sayings, you were...?'

'Yes, well the thing is...' he trailed off, his face losing all colour. He swayed a little and shook his head slightly. 'You'll have to excuse me. I'm not feeling well, this damn flu. I think I'll go lie down for a while.'

Alice came around the end of the kitchen bench and put her hand on his arm. 'You're not looking the best, Owen. Would you like me to call Janice?'

Janice was the retirement village's nurse. Her office was discretely located at the back of Alice's apartment building. Any visit to the nurse was usually fuel for the gossips tongues so tucking the office away allowed for private consultations to remain private.

'No, no,' Owen said. 'I'm absolutely fine apart from this damn flu. I just need to lie down for a while.'

'Is the reason for your visit urgent?' Alice asked

Owen's face closed down as he considered her question, then with a small frown he shook his head.

'Look, it's probably nothing at all.' He laughed. 'I guess it was just something nagging at me, and I knew you were up and had the best tea selection in the village. It's fine.' He waved a dismissive hand.

Alice helped him to his feet and they shuffled to the door, where she told him to wait. On a small round wooden table next to the door was a phone with direct lines to reception, the nurse, the kitchen, and counsellor. Apparently old people got depressed, according to Silvermoon management. Alice wasn't an advocate for telling other people your problems unless there was alcohol involved.

That was a by-product of raising a child alone in the fifties and sixties. Her motto for most of her life was "just shut up and get on with it".

She punched the button for reception. It was answered instantly.

'Yes, Ms Atkinson?'

'Vanessa dear, get someone to help Owen back to his room will you? He's in my apartment.'

'Really?'

'That's enough sass from you or I'll tell your boyfriend about the looks you've been giving Craig from the gardening staff.'

Vanessa laughed. 'I'll be right up.'

Thirty seconds later there was a soft knock and Alice opened the door. Vanessa was in her early twenties, with long brown hair and green eyes that winked at Alice when she saw her hand on Owen's arm. Smartly dressed in a dark green uniform, her name tag read Vanessa Carson, with the rather grand title of Concierge underneath.

'Come on, Mr Struthers. Let's help you on your walk of shame.'

'Oh really,' Alice said indignantly, but her smile ruined it. She was fond of Vanessa.

'I do want to talk to you, Alice,' Owen said to her. 'How about we have dinner later if I'm feeling better?'

Alice did her best to ignore another Vanessa wink and nodded. 'Of course. Get in touch if you're feeling better.' She watched them walk to the elevator. Owen's apartment was in the second building, which loomed over the main one. Twice the length and with an extra floor, it was home to the majority of residents.

'Vanessa?' Alice called as they disappeared into the elevator.

Her head popped back into view. 'I'll let you know when he's back home safely.'

'Thanks, and –'

'I'll set up a Dora.'

Alice smiled as the elevator doors closed. Dora Simmonds was a resident who had lain sick in her apartment for two days, too dazed and confused to call anyone and, because her family lived out of the country, no one had checked on her. The facility operated a policy of discretion, leaving residents alone unless they asked. No one here needed full time care, so it generally worked. Except in Dora's case. When they finally found her she was dehydrated and starving but had fully recovered. Since then management had asked all residents to check in every two days, but some of the staff had a more informal system. If they knew someone wasn't feeling well they'd arrange to pop in on them at least twice a day. They called it 'a Dora', much to the real Dora's chagrin.

Alice made a mental note to leave a tip for Vanessa at the end of the week. Then, because her mental note system wasn't as reliable as it used to be, she wrote it on a piece of paper and pinned it to the fridge with a magnet. Her fridge was covered in souvenir magnets. The few people she allowed into her home assumed they were from places around the world that she had visited, and technically they were. Alice had travelled far and wide in her working life, and each magnet represented a place she had visited, and a job successfully completed. It had been an exciting life, and as she studied the different shapes and colours it occurred to her that what she really missed, was working.

She was too old to get back into it. She couldn't trust her body, and although she was still more with-it mentally than many people her age, she wasn't as sharp as she had been fifty years ago. One rule about the con game was always be the smartest person in the room (and if you aren't the smartest, then be the most cunning).

It was mid-January. The morning was mild and bright, so Alice decided to go for a walk. Vanessa was behind the front desk and they exchanged waves before Alice exited through the doors of the main building, otherwise sarcastically referred to by residents as Colonel Mustard due to its colour. She went down the stairs, and onto the driveway. Turning left would take her along the tree-lined drive to the front gate. Instead, she crossed to the paved path, turned right and followed its curved direction around Colonel Mustard. She nodded to two residents who were pulling weeds out of the community vegetable garden. Up ahead she spied Betty going through the door to the Wellbeing Centre, which was a fancy name for a place designed to keep your head and body from decaying too quickly. Residents had named it the Olympic Complex. She called out, but her friend didn't acknowledge her as she disappeared inside. Alice didn't think anything of it. Half the people here had some form of hearing difficulty. But Alice thought Betty had looked worried.

She stopped outside the complex and peered through the large window. No one was in the small heated pool. Beyond that she could make out the back of a figure on one of the treadmills. It made no sense to her. They had to walk to get to a machine that walked for them. There was no sign of Betty, so maybe she was in the gaming room (the name of which had excited Alice when she'd first arrived, only to find that it was a room with cards and board games rather than casino activities).

Alice hesitated, unsure whether to continue her walk or go in search of her friend. It was Tuesday, wasn't it? Alice and Betty had a regular coffee date at 10am on Tuesdays. She would talk to Betty then.

Continuing on the path, she looped past Charlie's, the small café just for village residents, where she saw Teresa deep in conversation with a woman Alice didn't recognise.

She marched the length of Owen's building, which was officially called Rimu House, and unofficially nicknamed Stumpy, rounded the corner and ended up where she started. Pausing on the top step, she leaned against one of the concrete columns (which seemed to be there for no reason other than to say "hey look how pretentious this building is"). She listened to her breath rattling. At least it showed she was alive, she thought, even as the disquieting thought crept in that it didn't sound quite right.

She pulled her phone from her jersey pocket and went to dial Amanda's number. She stopped. Her granddaughter was working, which meant calls to her were in case of emergency only. A vague feeling that something, somewhere might not be alright didn't constitute an emergency. Alice shoved the phone back into her pocket and slunk inside, ignoring Vanessa's greeting as the elevator doors slid shut.

'I guess ignoring people is catching,' she mumbled to herself.

In her apartment she stripped off the extra layers, made herself another cup of tea, and checked her emails. Most of the people she knew were dead or lived in the village, so she didn't get many messages. Someone had emailed to warn her that her computer had been hacked and someone had videos of her watching pornography which was quite amusing; someone else wanted to give her millions of dollars in gold, which made her want to respond to say if she wanted gold she'd steal it.. Mostly Alice used the email account as an alternative way to keep in touch with Amanda, but there was nothing from her. After her daughter Carol passed away, Alice took Amanda in and raised her to be smart, cunning, and independent. There was never any need to worry when Amanda was working. Which is why Alice only worried a little bit.

A few minutes before ten Alice walked down to Charlie's. The day had warmed up since her early morning walk and she stopped on the path to remove her jersey before arriving just in time to see Betty approaching from the other direction.

'Morning, Alice,' Betty said with a smile.

'It certainly is,' Alice replied with a grin, which turned into a laugh when Betty rolled her eyes.

Betty wore jeans and an apricot-coloured jersey. Her battered brown bag was slung over one shoulder.

Charlie's was small, comfortable and, most importantly, warm and quiet. A while back, when Alice had gone into Wellington city to meet Amanda, she'd found the cafes too noisy for conversation. Luckily Amanda knew of a quiet out of the way place where the only noise was their voices and the occasional hiss of a coffee machine. Here there was a gentle buzz of voices without any fighting for dominance. Three of the six tables were occupied, two by complex staff, and the other by Les and Freda, a couple Alice knew had been married for fifty years. As she watched, while Les was focused on topping up his cup from the teapot, his wife casually reached up and switched off her hearing aid. When Les looked back and resumed his discourse on the problem with society his wife nodded as if agreeing with everything.

At the counter Betty surprised her by saying, 'Order what you like Alice, my shout.'

Alice was about to respond that it was her turn to buy, but she paused when she saw how intently Betty was studying the selection of scones. Normally Betty was strict with schedules, whose turn it was to do things, what time to show up, what to bring. They had met for a coffee every Tuesday for eight months, always alternating who paid. This was the first time Betty had muddled up the order. For a moment Alice wondered if she herself had mistaken whose turn it was to pay, but she distinctly remembered Betty paying for her savoury scone and herbal tea exactly one week ago.

Determined to find out what had caused the lapse in routine, Alice told the man behind the counter her order, then sat down at one of the empty tables.

'I suppose you're wondering why I'm paying two weeks in a row,' Betty said when she joined Alice.

Alice nodded. That she realised the change was a good sign. Betty wasn't cracking up.

'There's no problem I promise you.'

'You looked a little worried this morning,' Alice replied.

'I didn't see you this morning.'

'I was out for a walk and I saw you go into the Olympic complex. You seemed preoccupied.'

Betty waved her hand. 'Ah I see. I was going for a workout with Peter and he told me last time he was going to try a new exercise with me. I guess I was nervous about it. I'm not used to exercise that doesn't involve moving livestock.'

Their scones arrived and they both smiled. Alice had chosen a cheese one with a small dollop of butter on the side, while Betty had gone for the more adventurous date and herb scone. The café had a suggestion box on the counter and every week they made one of the combinations suggested by residents. There had been some very interesting results, not all of them successful. Alice wasn't convinced about date and herb.

While they cut and buttered and sampled tiny bites, Alice considered why her friend was lying to her.

THREE

There might be another explanation of course, but a career of dealing with liars and thieves made Alice assume that everyone was lying until proven otherwise. She knew for a fact that Peter wasn't working that day. She'd run into him the previous evening and he'd mentioned he was taking Tuesday off to get a spray tan. Peter had been training for a body building competition and apparently getting his skin painted deep brown was part of the preparation process. Alice had never been a fan of artificial colouring, but she had to admit his muscles looked pretty good, even if she had to suppress a surprising urge to tell him to put some clothes on every time she saw him striding around the complex in shorts and a singlet.

She realised her thoughts were wandering and reigned them in while sipping the milky foam off the top of her drink. Betty had quickly moved on to talking about how Gordon had behaved in the dining room the night before. Alice nodded to show she was listening, which she wasn't.

Maybe it was nothing. Maybe Betty was secretly meeting a man (or a woman which, thanks to her granddaughter, didn't shock her as much as it may once have done). Maybe her friend was simply confused and her own mind was too used to nefarious explanations for simple behaviour. She smiled ruefully and tried to focus on the conversation.

'...honestly don't know why he bothers. We've all said no to him at one time or another. He reminds me of this ram we once had on the farm. He wouldn't leave the ewes alone. Would always find a way through the fence and start harassing them.'

'What did you do?' Alice asked.

'Took away his reason for visiting,' Betty replied, using her fingers to mimic scissors.

Alice shuddered. The closest she'd ever been to farm life was once staying at a bed and breakfast where the owners had three chickens and a pet goat. She preferred animals that were small and self-sufficient. Silvermoon had a resident cat that was constantly scamming food from the residents. Alice had once watched the little brown and white cat gobble up a bowl of food she'd left out for it, then walk straight to another door and meow pitifully until a second bowl was produced.

The staff called her Maddy.

Alice called her a hustler. She approved.

'...don't know what they are going to do about Gordon. Honestly, I've complained to management twice about him and they don't do anything.'

Alice looked at her friend, thinking it was ironic she'd used the word honestly twice while Alice believed she was lying about something.

'Did you know Owen is sick?' Alice said in the brief silence, while Betty sipped her drink.

'How sick?'

Alice smiled at her sharp tone.

Betty caught her expression and screwed up her face. 'I'm just concerned,' she grumbled. 'The same way I'd be worried if you were sick.'

'Not quite the same way.'

Betty shuffled in her chair and picked at the remains of her scone. 'Maybe not exactly the same.'

Alice nodded. Those words confirmed one thing and ruled out another. Betty wasn't the sort to cheat on someone so whatever she was lying about didn't have anything to do with a man.

'Perhaps I should check in on him,' Betty glanced at her watch.

'I'm sure he'll be alright, Betty. I spoke to Vanessa this morning. There's a Dora in place.'

Her friend's face betrayed her conflict and she picked up and put down her bag several times.

'Oh for goodness sake. Just go.'

Betty's face relaxed in relief and she was out of her seat in an instant as if afraid her friend would rescind the offer.

'I'll see you later, Alice.'

'Remember the big game tomorrow,' Alice called as Betty hustled out.

Unlike their more intimate game, the annual Silvermoon Village Poker Tournament was played for prestige rather than wealth. For Alice, it wasn't about the shiny trophy the winner got to flaunt for a year. Nor was it about the side bets that occurred between residents. For Alice, it was purely bragging rights, and a clear sign that she could still outthink and outwit a bunch of retired office workers and housewives. She had won the tournament for the past two years and knew there were some murmurings amongst the other competitors that she should be banned from future events. She had heard that several had looked her up on the internet, convinced she used to be a professional gambler. The thought had her grinning into her coffee.

'You look pleased with yourself, Alice,' Les called out.

'Leave her be,' his wife scolded.

'You haven't won that trophy yet you know,' Les said with a stern expression on his face. 'I've been practicing every day for the last month and I'm feeling confident.'

'Care to make it interesting?' Alice replied.

'No, he wouldn't,' Freda said before he could open his mouth.

Alice left the remains of her scone on the table and the bickering voices in her ears as she walked outside. Les was a good man, a little too self-important, and that was why he would never win the trophy. He always adopted a smug expression whenever he had a good hand, and his eyes darted to wherever his wife was sitting in the room when he was bluffing.

The warm sun on her face and ceaseless cheerfulness of the bird-filled trees around her convinced Alice that she might have been mistaken about Betty lying to her. She took the long way back to her apartment, and by the time she walked through her front door she had almost forgotten it.

Almost.

Which was a mistake.

FOUR

On Wednesday, the poker tournament started at exactly 10am in the communal room. This year there were twenty players vying for the title, with an equal number of spectators. The players were split into four tables of five. Each table would play until a single player had won all the chips. Then the top players would assemble at one table to decide the overall winner. It was usually over by lunchtime, when the trophy was officially awarded to the winner by Tracey Miller, the manager of the complex. After which, Silvermoon put on a light lunch of sandwiches and cakes for everyone.

As they were milling around waiting, Vanessa sidled up next to Alice.

'Owen is feeling better.'

'I see that, dear.'

Owen was standing in a small cluster of people on the other side of the room. He still looked a little pale, but appeared much better than the previous day. Betty was glued to his side, ready to offer a steadying hand if needed.

'Of course you do,' Vanessa said, her eyes conveying the laughter she was suppressing. 'He was a bit brighter yesterday at dinner time. I don't think Betty has left his side since yesterday morning, so a Dora wasn't really necessary.' This time she did laugh, and dropped a wink in for good measure.

Alice snorted. 'Really, Vanessa. You ought to worry more about your own sex life and less about other peoples.'

'Unfortunately mine is on hold. Ben is away for a couple of weeks on some work thing, so it's just me and the roommate at home eating ice cream and binging on Netflix.'

'What's a Netflix?'

'You don't know about Netflix? Oh Alice, you should get it. It's amazing.'

A small bell rang to signal that the players should to go to their tables. Alice sat down opposite Les, who's face suggested he wasn't as confident as he'd stated the day before. On his left was a retired army general by the name of Gavin. They'd tried calling him General Gavin but the first stern look from him put paid to that. To his right was Sofia, a retired dance teacher whose body vibrated with excitement at everything, as if the very act of being alive charged her with electricity.

The fifth player took her seat and Alice thought it was good that she was already in poker mode, otherwise her surprise might have shown. She didn't know this woman, although she had seen her the day before with Teresa at Charlie's.

'Nanci Katz,' the woman smiled and shoved her hand out.

'Alice,' she replied, briefly but firmly shaking the offered hand.

She studied the newcomer while Nanci introduced herself to the others at the table. She was young, in her early seventies, with light coloured hair. There was a bit of padding to her face now, but Alice could see the beauty that would have had men drooling a few decades earlier.

A new player certainly made life interesting from a poker perspective, but it also raised some questions. And it changed Alice's game strategy. Her original plan had been to win as much as possible early on so she could take a break and watch the other tables. However now she would have to be more cautious, at least until she understood how Nanci played.

'...moved in?' Les was asking.

'No, I'm here for a week teaching sculpting classes to the residents and Tracey graciously said I could sit in and play. Not that I really know what I'm doing I'm afraid, solitaire is the limit of my card experience.'

Alice smiled. In her experience anyone who proclaimed a lack of knowledge on a subject was either exaggerating or outright lying. The obvious explanation of course was that Nanci genuinely didn't know anything about poker, but Alice hadn't often dealt with those types of people through the years. Honest people.

Regardless, the first few hands would tell her everything she needed to know.

She suddenly realised everyone at the table had gone quiet and were looking at her. 'Sorry, what?'

'I asked how you got so good at poker?' Nanci repeated.

'How do you know I'm good?'

'Pretty hard to miss it.' Nanci gestured to the plaque hanging on the wall next to the door, clearly showing Alice's name in the list of tournament winners.

'Of course,' Alice smiled, inwardly cursing herself. She preferred being the one pointing out the obvious, not the other way around. 'Well, I've had a slightly longer life than most of you, it gives me an advantage in some areas.'

'Life experience gives us everything, am I right?' Nanci looked at the others around the table and they all nodded enthusiastically.

Like getting up five times a night to pee, Alice thought.

Vanessa sat down in the remaining chair. Alice exchanged a smile with her before looking around to see Silvermoon staff taking their places at the other tables. Officially they were there to make sure the game ran smoothly. Unofficially, Vanessa had confided, they were supposed to stamp out the more obvious cheating.

Each player had an identical pile of chips in front of them. Yellow were worth one dollar, blue two dollars, red five dollars, and the black chips were ten dollars. Vanessa unwrapped a deck of cards and shuffled them with practised ease.

'You're getting quite good at that,' Gavin commented.

'Thank you, Gavin,' she replied. Her mouth twitched and Alice wondered if she was remembering their secret sessions where Alice had taught her tricks to impress her friends and win rent money.

Alice was of the opinion that every young woman needed a skill they could pull out of their back pocket, one that might come in handy in unforeseen circumstances.

Vanessa dealt the first hand and all other thoughts were pushed aside as Alice focussed on the game. She folded and sat back to watch what the others did. Les pushed forward two blue chips, then his eyes turned to where Freda was sitting in a chair under the window, her head in a book. Alice had already noted her location before they started. Les, for all his practicing, was a creature of habit. And he was bluffing. Sure enough when he finally showed his cards all he had was a pair of twos.

As the game progressed, Alice was pleased to see that the other players still had the same tells as well. The only one she was having trouble reading was Nanci. The woman lost as much as she won, and she didn't seem to have any obvious gestures or ticks that showed.

In no time at all Gavin was throwing his cards down and pushing his chair away from the table.

'Well done, all. A very enjoyable way to spend the morning.' He nodded briskly then walked, straight backed, over to the refreshments table to make himself a hot drink.

By the time Sofia bowed out ten minutes later, Alice had concluded that Nanci was as she appeared: a novice at poker. Nanci soon joined the others on the sideline and it was just Alice and Les left at the table. Alice's pile of chips was much bigger than Les's and he had taken to mopping his forehead with a large blue handkerchief.

Forty minutes after they started it was all over. Les pushed all his chips into the middle of the table and snuck a furtive look at his wife. Alice decided not to fold after all, and won the hand, and the table, with a pair of fours.

Les tried his best to hide his disappointment, and for the first time Alice felt a twinge of guilt.

It's not like I'm taking his money, she argued with herself.

'Well done again, Alice,' Les said.

'Thanks. I guess the coffees are on me at the café tomorrow, Les.'

His expression brightened at the mention of a free drink, and when she glanced over to him later he was cheerfully recounting his game to an increasingly bored-looking Freda.

'Normal programming then,' Vanessa said from across the table.

'Eh?'

'You winning. As expected.'

'I don't know about expected,' Alice replied, 'but it certainly beats the alternative.'

Vanessa grinned, then went in search of a drink. Alice knew she would be back to serve as dealer for the final game. She stood up slowly, her back stiff from sitting for so long. Her first few steps were tottering, but once blood started to flow everything eased and she moved more freely. She stopped by the refreshment table for a handful of chips, briefly eyeing up the cheese before dismissing it. Dairy products were problematic these days, and she only braved her beloved camembert on very special occasions.

Only one table was still playing. It was down to Teresa and Lawrence, a short man with an equally short temper. Alice had been glad not to have him at her table. Last year when he lost, he'd swept the chips off the table and stomped out of the room, refusing to speak to anyone for several days.

Teresa lay down her cards, revealing a full house of queens and tens. Everyone held their breath and looked to Lawrence. He shrugged, offered his hand in congratulations, and wandered off.

'I hear he's been told by his doctor that his blood pressure is so high he won't see another Christmas if he doesn't keep his temper in check,' Betty said.

Alice looked at her friend. 'It's not like you to gossip.'

'It's not gossip if it's true,' Betty replied.

Alice was about to argue the point when she spotted something curious. At least to her. Teresa had stood up from the table and was walking around the room, smiling, looking around her a little too much to be normal. Finally she stood next to Nanci. Teresa spoke to her briefly and a few seconds later both women disappeared through the door to the hallway.

'What are you looking at?'

'I'm not sure,' Alice admitted. 'But I have a feeling something is going on.'

'What?'

Alice frowned. 'I can't be sure. I'm suspicious by nature and I have a thought.'

'Thinking at our age is dangerous,' Betty laughed, slipping her arm through Alice's.

'It keeps me young,' Alice smiled.

'And being suspicious?'

'Kept me out of jail a few times.'

Betty's smile faltered, as if unsure whether Alice was being serious. Then she laughed and Alice joined her.

A bell rang indicating the start of the final round. Four players took their seats, but Teresa hadn't come back. Vanessa sat down and behind her, Tracey looked at her watch and tapped her foot. Alice had always found the woman a little officious. Tracey liked everything to run on time, which didn't work when you were dealing with children, animals, or stubborn old people.

As Tracey opened her mouth to speak, Alice reached out for her drink, accidentally sweeping her pile of chips onto the floor.

'Oh my goodness, I am so sorry,' Alice said to the table.

'Oh for–' Tracey stifled the rest of her sentence. She gestured for Vanessa to help pick up the mess.

'Oh my goodness?' Vanessa muttered as she knelt next to Alice's chair and began to collect the coloured chips.

'I refuse to win by default,' Alice whispered back.

'Oh my goodness, no,' Vanessa winked. She placed the chips back on the table and Alice had them sorted into piles by the time Vanessa had retaken her seat.

Luckily, before Tracey said anything further, Teresa came back through the door and took her seat.

'I'm so sorry. I was in the bathroom,' Teresa said, an excuse that shut down any potential comments about tardiness by anyone.

'Let's begin,' Tracey said, tapping Vanessa on the shoulder.

It didn't take long for Alice to realise that there was a new level of skill in her friend's poker playing that hadn't been there the week before. Teresa won three of the first four hands, once by bluffing, which Alice had not picked up on.

With renewed concentration Alice focused on the game.

And lost, badly.

Judging by the complete silence in the room, she wasn't the only one shocked by this result. Vanessa's mouth looked like she was readying to swallow an entire watermelon. Betty's face showed a similar reaction, and Owen's eyebrows were trying to meet his receding hairline. Amongst the shocked faces were the smiles of those Alice had beaten, this year and previously. Les's smile was the widest.

'Congratulations, Teresa,' Alice said.

'Thanks, Alice.' Teresa couldn't hide her delight, but she could barely meet Alice's eyes.

'That was the best I've ever seen you play,' Owen told Teresa, and Alice was pleased that *she* hadn't said it, though they were all thinking it. She didn't want to come across as bitter and she really was happy for Teresa. But her gut and Teresa's flushed cheeks suggested there was definitely something up.

'Ladies and gentlemen, if I could have some quiet?' Tracey said in a loud voice. She was holding the small trophy the winners got to keep.

After the brief presentation some people returned to their rooms, while others made their way to the refreshments table.

'Better luck next year,' Gavin said as he filled a coffee cup.

'I guarantee things will be different next year,' Alice replied. She was determined to learn the source of Teresa's sudden poker skills and she had a feeling it had something to do with Nanci.

A crashing sound startled her. Turning, she saw Betty slumped over a table, not moving.

'Betty!' Owen rushed from across the room. Alice hustled over as he attempted to lift Betty into a chair, but she slipped from his grip and fell back down.

'Betty? Are you alright?' Alice said, bending over to look at her face.

Betty's eyes stared back, unseeing. For a brief moment Alice hoped that it was just a fall, but when she pressed her fingers onto Betty's wrist in search of a pulse she couldn't find it.

Betty was gone.

FIVE

Death was a shock. Even in a place where the average age of the residents was in the high seventies. But it wasn't unheard of, and it didn't take long for the standard protocols of the Silvermoon Retirement Village to spring into action. The first step was to usher everyone out of the room, which they did successfully. Almost. Alice refused to leave her friend, and when Owen heard she was staying he insisted on staying as well. Teresa made a half-hearted protest too, but her face was pale and it didn't take much persuasion for her to go and have a lie down. Alice promised to pop by her apartment later to check on her.

Soon they were the only people left in the room apart from Tracey and Vanessa, who was on the phone arranging for an ambulance. Alice had always considered ambulances for the living, but the cynical side of her saw the reason behind the summons. No one wants to be the one to pronounce the death of a person. Or more importantly, to get it wrong. However in this case Alice was quite certain

Betty was gone. She hadn't moved an inch and her eyes still had the same lifeless stare.

'I really think it would be best for the two of you to wait somewhere else until we can get this...' Tracey trailed off.

'Sorted?' Alice completed her sentence. 'This is Betty. My friend. She is not something to get sorted. You understand?'

Tracey's cheeks reddened. 'I was merely suggesting, for your sake– '

'I'm staying. We're staying.' Alice turned to Owen who was sitting in a chair next to Betty holding her hand.

'It's funny, really. I was very fond of her, and was going to tell her. One day. Oh, who am I kidding? I was married for fifty years and I still get tongue tied when it comes to talking about my feelings.'

'Which is why your wife was a saint,' Alice replied.

Owen smiled ruefully. 'Most likely. I shall miss her.' He looked down at the hand he was holding and Alice followed his eyes.

She frowned. There was something about Betty's fingernails that didn't seem quite right. She bent down to take a closer look. Her fingernails had white lines across them. It triggered a memory somewhere in the back of Alice's mind, but she couldn't pin it down.

A hand touched her shoulder. 'The ambulance will be here shortly, Alice. I need to go and find her file so Tracey can let her next of kin know.' Vanessa squatted next to her. 'Do you need anything?'

Alice started to shake her head, then glanced across to Owen who was staring into nothingness. 'I think a situation like this calls for more than tea, don't you?'

'You know alcohol isn't allowed in the common areas.'

'Exceptional circumstances. Stop by my place on the way back. In the kitchen cabinet above the oven is a small silver flask.'

Vanessa nodded. 'Be back as soon as I can.' She gave Alice's arm a quick squeeze then headed out of the room.

Alice was turning her attention back to Betty's fingernails when Tracey blurted, 'I'm sorry about the loss of your friend.'

Privately Alice thought she should have said this earlier, but outwardly she nodded her thanks.

The door swung open and a stern young woman strode in. She looked in her early thirties, with short black hair, and was dressed in tight fitting jeans and a dark blue T-shirt.

'Judith? What are you doing here?'

Judith's eyes seemed to dart around the room, as if taking a series of mental pictures.

'We were supposed to meet for coffee when the tournament finished, remember? What's going on here, Aunt Tracey?'

'This poor woman has passed away.'

The way Judith's expression changed made Alice wonder about the sudden interest. She picked her way through the gaps between the tables and stopped next to her aunt.

'Suspicious?'

Tracey snorted. 'Judith, there are never suspicious deaths here. Few places have a higher death rate than retirement villages. It's the nature of the business. No offence,' she added, looking at Alice and Owen.

'That's why I came here,' Alice said, earning her a puzzled expression from Tracey before understanding dawned and she looked away with a red face.

'Mmm,' Judith replied. 'Judith Miller, detective, Wellington police.'

'Alice Atkinson, retired, Silvermoon Retirement Village.'

Judith's mouth twitched at the edges. 'Sorry, the detective thing is new. I'm still trying it on for size.'

'Congratulations,' Alice said. 'It seems to fit reasonably well.'

Another twitch of the mouth. 'If you don't mind me saying you seem to be taking this woman's death well.'

'Her name is Betty,' Owen said.

'I'm almost a century old,' Alice replied. 'You don't get this far without burying a lot of loved ones. You tend to become... pragmatic about death.'

'Alice!' Owen looked shocked.

She patted him on the arm. 'Of course I'm going to miss her.'

Judith seemed about to say something, but stopped herself, shifting her look between Owen and Tracey.

Vanessa returned, holding a folder. 'I've got the contact information for you.' She handed a slip of paper to Tracey, carefully filling the space between her and Alice. Sliding a small object out of her pants pocket, Vanessa held it behind her. Alice took the flask in her lap and covered it with both hands.

'Thank you, Vanessa. I'll need to go make some calls. Judith, would you mind waiting here? I won't be long.'

Judith waved a hand and sat down in a chair at the adjoining table. Tracey pulled her phone out and began dialling as she left the room.

'Vanessa, why don't you open a window,' Alice suggested. 'It's a little warm in here. Owen, would you mind giving her a hand? You know how the latches stick, I'm sure she could use a man's assistance.'

Owen seemed about to refuse, but chivalry overcame reluctance and he gently placed Betty's hand on the table and stood up.

Alice quickly poured a few drops from the flask into Owen's tea while everyone was distracted. Then she turned to Judith. 'Go on.'

'Eh?'

'You want to practice by looking at this as a crime scene. So go ahead.'

'How did you know?'

'I may not know how to post something on that Faces book, but I know people.'

'You don't mind? It's your friend.'

'Yes, she's my friend, but unless you're planning to autopsy her on the poker table, a close inspection isn't going to hurt.'

Judith jumped up from her seat and bent over Betty's body, clasping her hands behind her back as if the act of being near a recently deceased person would prove too much temptation and she was afraid she would poke and prod. Her stance reminded Alice of a chicken bending forward to peck at the ground.

'Deceased seems to be in her early seventies, approximately fifty kilograms,' Judith murmured. 'No medical bracelets indicating any known conditions. Did she...?' Judith turned her head to look at Alice.

'She'd spent her working life on the farm so she'd led a healthier life than most of us. She had some blood pressure problems, but that was it as far as I know.'

'And she fell?'

Alice frowned as she tried to recall everything that happened before Betty died. 'I think so. I had my back to her and heard a sudden bang, but before that she seemed fine.'

Judith nodded and resumed her inspection. Finally she stretched up tall. 'I'm sorry for your loss.'

'Thank you. You don't think it's suspicious then?'

A troubled look came across Judith's face, as if she wasn't sure whether she was being mocked. Alice made sure to keep her expression neutral.

'Difficult to tell without an autopsy, which is unlikely in these circumstances, but there's no outward sign of trauma so I think it's safe to say she died of natural causes.' Judith gave a little smile. 'Sorry, that sounds really officious.'

'Is speaking like that part of your training?'

'Actually, yes it is.'

'What are you two talking about?' Owen asked as he rejoined them.

'Just filling in time,' Alice replied, wishing he'd given them ten more seconds. She couldn't ask a police detective to look at Betty's fingernails now without awkward questions or upsetting Owen.

Soon the room got very busy.

First Tracey came back in, almost immediately followed by two ambulance staff. Then Owen insisted on accompanying them to wherever it was they took the recently deceased, and finally Tracey began quietly berating Judith for being disrespectful and treating Betty's death as a training exercise. For a moment everyone forgot about Alice. Sometimes she found if she sat still she became almost invisible, which was on occasion very useful.

She beckoned Vanessa over. 'Do you have your phone?' she whispered.

'Sure,' Vanessa replied in matching volume.

'Can you take a picture of Betty's fingernails.'

It was obvious by her face that Vanessa had questions, but rather than ask them she pulled out her phone, then looked at all the people crowding the body.

'Leave it to me,' Alice said. She stood up and took a few paces over to the adjoining table.

'Oh dear,' she said loudly, slumping into a chair. Everyone ignored her. 'OH DEAR,' she shouted.

Heads turned and conversations paused and suddenly she was the centre of attention.

'It's all too much. Another friend gone,' she wailed.

Tracey and Owen immediately stepped towards her.

'When will it all end?' Alice continued. 'Why must they be taken before their time?'

'Before their time?' Tracey repeated.

Now everyone was shuffling towards Alice, the ambulance staff looking a lot more excited about a *living* patient.

'Are you alright, Alice?' Owen's face was filled with concern and she felt guilty.

Behind everyone she saw Vanessa give a thumbs up.

'I'm fine. Just silly.' She sat up straight. 'It just became too much for a moment. I think I'd better go and lie down.'

'Of course,' Tracey said. 'Vanessa, will you escort Alice back to her apartment please.'

'Yes, Tracey. Come on, Alice.' Vanessa helped Alice to her feet. They were in the elevator before Alice let go of her arm.

'Are you going to tell me what's going on?' Vanessa asked.

'Do you know how to google?'

Vanessa grinned. 'Alice, I'm a millennial. You might as well ask me if I know how to breathe.'

'Good, because Betty didn't die of natural causes.'

'What?'

'She was poisoned.'

SIX

'What do you mean she was poisoned?'

They were sitting on the couch in Alice's apartment.

'Show me the picture of her fingernails.'

Vanessa pulled her phone out and tapped and swiped until a picture filled the screen.

'See those lines?' Alice said pointing to them.

'Oh yeah, that doesn't look right.'

'I don't think it is right. I've got this vague memory of lines like that but I can't recall exactly. Can you look up the possible causes of those lines on the google?'

On her phone, Vanessa brought up a search box. She typed in 'lines on fingernails' and selected the first item. They both scanned the article.

'It says here that slight vertical ridges commonly develop in older adults,' Vanessa said.

'That's the opening sentence, Vanessa. Read faster. It also says deep horizontal ridges may indicate a serious condition.'

'Health condition, not poison. You can't really believe Betty was poisoned.'

'I'm not sure what to think,' she admitted. 'But what if Betty's death *was* murder. No one is going to look into it. Everyone is convinced that it's just a case of another old person dying.'

'Murder?! Alice, that's crazy. Why would anyone want to murder Betty?'

Alice looked out the window at the leaves on the trees swaying a little in the breeze. It made them seem alive. 'I don't know.'

'Exactly.'

'But I'd be the first to admit I don't know everything. It couldn't hurt to ask a few questions.' She turned back to Vanessa. 'You said yourself, not much is going on at home, so you can help me.'

Vanessa dropped her gaze to her hands, turning her phone over and over. 'You don't think this has anything to do with...'

'With what?'

'Well, you've seemed a little bored lately, since you helped that writer out. Sort of... restless. Twitchy. You don't think you might be looking for things that aren't there? Just to do something exciting?' She looked at Alice, sadness and embarrassment mixing on her face.

Alice bit off the retort that sprang to her lips. Vanessa was right, she was bored.

But that wasn't it.

She patted Vanessa on the leg. 'You could be right. Maybe this whole thing will be a complete waste of time. So let's pretend it's a game, just between you and I. Humour me.'

Alice could tell Vanessa still wasn't convinced but she nodded. 'Where do we start?'

'We need to talk to everyone that was in the room and build up a picture of what Betty was doing just before she died.'

'Okay, I think I remember most of the people.'

'Why don't you go back to work. Tracey might be looking for you. Write down a list of everyone, and let's meet back here at the end of your shift. I'll shout for pizza.'

'I thought pizza gave you gas?'

'Honey, everything gives me gas these days.'

'TMI,' Vanessa leapt up and headed for the door.

'One more thing.' Alice waited for Vanessa to turn. 'There's a difference between humouring me and patronising me. Understand?' She realised the words would sound harsh so she tried to keep her tone light.

Vanessa's face flushed and she shrugged. 'Fair enough. See you soon.' This time she made it all the way to the door before she paused. 'Alice? Are you okay? About Betty.'

'I was fond of her and I shall miss her quite a lot, once I've had a chance to think about it. So let's delay that for a while, shall we?'

Vanessa nodded and disappeared through the door.

Alice got to her feet and went into the kitchen. She opened the cupboard next to the fridge and shifted a canister of flour. Tucked away in the back corner was a second silver hip flask.

She unscrewed the lid and sniffed the whiskey inside. Technically she wasn't supposed to be drinking with all the medication her doctor made her take. But if ever there was a time to break that rule it was now. Alice took a swig, swirling the liquid in her mouth, letting it kick all her taste buds into live before swallowing.

Her lips trembled slightly and she felt the corners of her eyes moisten. Alice took another drink. At least she could blame the alcohol for this uncharacteristic display of emotion.

Maybe this was more about her than Betty. She hoped that she was wrong, that Betty's death was natural. But she owed it to her friend to find out the truth. And if Betty's death wasn't natural, then someone was going to be in a lot of trouble.

SEVEN

The trouble with secret investigations was that you were prevented from asking a lot of the more obvious questions. Like, "did you know anyone who wanted Betty dead?"

Luckily Alice had spent a lifetime perfecting the skill of getting information out of people without them realising it. It was very useful, especially in the age of computers, where stealing passwords was often required before you could steal anything else (though Alice was mostly retired by the time computers really took off). However before she could ask any questions about Betty's death, Alice needed to ask one very important one. Which was why she was knocking on Owen's door.

He took a long time to open it and when he did his eyes were red and puffy. 'Hi Alice. Come in, please.'

He turned and she followed, closing the door behind her. His apartment was a smaller, although no less plush, version of hers. The biggest difference between the two were the mementos of his life scattered around the place. Framed pictures of family highlighting the passage of time, little knickknacks dotted along the windowsill and in the corner of the kitchen bench, and a truly hideous woollen rug underneath the coffee table. Alice had never been a knickknack type of person, she never saw the point, it was just another thing to dust or pack when you moved.

'Would you like a cup of tea?' Owen asked her.

She was about to say no, then thought it might be good for him to be busy so changed her mind. 'Yes please, but only if you'll have one too.'

He nodded absently and walked into the kitchen to switch the kettle on.

'How are you, Owen?' she asked as he busied himself with cups and milk and teaspoons.

'In a bit of shock, really. You know, I moved here when my wife died. We'd been married for fifty years and I didn't take her death terribly well. It was my children who suggested, insisted really, that I move in here. I think they wanted me to be around other people all the time so I didn't do anything silly.'

'Silly?' Alice asked.

'Oh, nothing permanent,' he shook his head. 'But you hear about it all the time, don't you? Married couples who have been together for so long, when one goes the other gives up. Not my sort of thing of course. I miss Karen very much, but life is like a job, you can't quit halfway through just because things get a little rocky.'

Alice nodded.

'Then I met Betty, and I grew fond of her, and I felt a little...'

'Guilty?'

Owen gave her a smile tinged with sadness. 'Yes, I suppose so. Anyway I think Betty felt the same, we hadn't really discussed it.'

'You mean you hadn't discussed it at all.'

'Well, no. You see it's been over half a century since I told a woman I was fond of her. I'm a bit out of practice.' He paused and straightened his tie a little before pouring the tea. 'Funny, really. I spent a lifetime working in offices, first hating the bosses, then admiring them, then copying them, and finally becoming them. I learned when to speak and when to listen and as a result I did fairly well for myself.'

Alice knew he was being modest. When he retired he had been the most successful CEO in the history of the bank, taking them to record profits and being universally admired.

'But talking to women in matters of the heart has always eluded me.' He smiled. 'Sounds a bit old fashioned doesn't it?'

'I hate to tell you this, Owen, but you're not exactly young anymore.'

'You can talk,' he shot back.

'A useful skill I've found,' she smiled back at him.

'Touché.' He handed her a cup of tea. 'Now be quiet and drink your tea.'

'Actually I wanted to ask you something. I was wondering if Betty had said anything to you about feeling unwell lately.'

Owen frowned and shook his head. 'No, but then she was the sort that didn't talk about her aches and pains. Remember last year with her ribs?'

She remembered well. Betty had cracked two of her ribs during a severe coughing fit, and lived with the pain for a week before going to the nurse. Not once had she complained and no one had noticed anything.

'I just wish she would have said something if she had been feeling ill. I wish I'd paid more attention to her today instead of worrying about poker.'

Owen patted the back of her hand. 'Don't you blame yourself. I spoke to her several times during the tournament and she looked and sounded fine. In fact she'd just made a friendly wager on you winning the whole thing.'

'Who did she make it with?' Alice asked.

'That new woman. What's her name now? Nanci?'

It was Alice's turn to frown. 'Who was Nanci betting on?'

'Teresa. Betty felt bad taking the bet, but not that bad, it was only for a hundred dollars, and she told me afterwards that anyone who bet on Teresa over you deserved to learn the hard way what a bad idea that was.'

Alice blew on her tea and took a sip, thinking. This woman's name kept popping up. Alice was beginning to have an inkling of how Teresa might have won the poker tournament, but to confirm it she would need to talk to both Teresa and Nanci. Besides, that had nothing to do with Betty's death.

'How are you feeling?' she asked.

'You already asked that,' Owen replied.

'I did? I mean physically. You weren't feeling well yesterday.'

He scratched his temple then shrugged. 'I feel fine. It must have been a 24 hour thing.'

'Good. At our age 24 hour things have a habit of developing into 24 day things, so I'm glad you're feeling better. Do you mind me asking what you wanted to talk to me about yesterday?'

Owen frowned and played with the knot of his tie. 'It doesn't really matter now.'

'Was it about Betty?' Alice guessed.

'Yes it was, but probably not how you think.'

Alice considered. If you dismissed matters of the heart then the next likely option was obvious. 'Money?'

'I did want your opinion on something, without going into the specifics, but now Betty has passed, circumstances have changed and I don't want to break confidences.'

Alice considered pressing the matter. If Betty had money problems it might point to a motive for her murder. She wasn't quite sure how but anything out of the ordinary might be relevant. She looked at the conflict on Owen's face and decided now wasn't the time.

'Of course. I completely understand.'

Owen's shoulders slumped a little and he let out a soft sigh. 'Do you think they'll tell us when they get hold of her children?'

'I'm sure they will. I would imagine Silvermoon will want to do some sort of memorial service here. And if they don't then we'll organise it ourselves.'

Owen was nodding. 'Yes good idea. Perhaps I should...'

'Why don't you leave it for today, Owen. Perhaps tomorrow you could start organising things. I'm sure Tracey would be more than happy for you to take the lead on this.'

He nodded again and Alice left him rummaging through a kitchen draw looking for a pad and pen.

Alice was halfway back to her place when Vanessa appeared from around a corner.

'Tracey gave me the rest of the day away from the front desk.'

'How did you arrange that?' Alice asked.

'I'm not sure I want to tell you,' Vanessa said, falling into step next to Alice.

Alice glanced at her. 'And yet I can tell you're dying to.'

'I may have told her I was worried about how you were taking Betty's death,' she grinned.

'Nice,' Alice replied.

'You don't sound surprised,' Vanessa said, disappointment obvious in her voice.

'It was the logical thing to say. Tracey would never have let you off work if you said you were upset by a resident's death, so it had to be one of us, and since you're helping me out it makes sense you used my name.'

She looked at Vanessa and added, 'but keep trying, one day you'll surprise me.'

'So where are we going, boss?'

'Back to my place. It's a bit early for pizza, but we can work on the list of who was in the room when Betty died. And for goodness sake can you slow down? These legs have seen a few more years than yours.'

Vanessa slowed and muttered an apology. Alice linked her arm with Vanessa's and they walked at a more leisurely pace back to her apartment.

'Let's see what our collective memories can recall,' Alice said once they were sitting on her couch. 'Here.' She held out a small pad and pencil, but Vanessa pulled her phone out instead.

'I can type faster than I can write,' she explained. 'Besides a tree died for that pad.'

'Well, it's already dead,' Alice waved the pad but Vanessa shook her head.

'What happens if I lose the paper?'

'What happens if you lose your phone?' Alice shot back.

Vanessa's face showed such genuine horror that Alice felt an urge to apologise and reassure her she was just joking.

'Alright, let's see. There was Gavin, Sofia, and Les at my table.' She paused as Vanessa's fingers sprinted across the screen of her phone. 'Then there—'

A knock at the door interrupted her.

Alice automatically reached for her phone to check the camera, then stopped herself. She trusted Vanessa, but only so far. As far as she knew Silvermoon management weren't aware of her extra security precautions and she preferred to keep it that way.

'I'll get it,' Vanessa said, jumping off the couch with energy that Alice hadn't felt in decades.

Alice was putting her phone back on the side table when she heard something that made her jaw clench.

'Hello, Mr Harrison. Come on in.'

Damn, she thought.

ƐIGHT

Gordon Harrison fancied himself the resident lothario. He had read somewhere that retirement villages were hotbeds for hook ups and that older people were experiencing a sexual revolution. Gordon wanted to be the poster boy for that revolution.

Alice knew he used to work for a government department, but she'd never had a long enough conversation to find out any more than that.

He wasn't aggressively pushy. Handsy? Yes. Relentless? Sometimes. Ever hopeful? Definitely. But he took every rejection with good grace. Even if it only resulted in a temporary reprieve for the lady in question.

When he stepped into her apartment, Gordon's slim body was clad in a pale blue tracksuit, with bright orange running shoes. What remained of his hair was slicked down with too much gel or something equally slimy, and dyed brown, which might have worked if he'd done the same with his bushy eyebrows and ever-present stubble, which were a more believable grey.

'Alice!' he exclaimed, as if surprised to see her sitting on her couch in her living room. 'I heard about Betty and I rushed right over to see how you were coping.'

It happened hours ago, she thought irritably. That's not rushing, even for this place.

Outwardly she smiled. 'Thank you, Gordon, I appreciate you stopping by.'

Gordon walked briskly over and took Vanessa's seat on the couch. He patted Alice's knee and she stifled an urge to break his finger.

'She was a lovely lady, Betty was. I didn't know her as well as I would have liked—'

I bet.

'But I know she was well-liked, and she always stopped to chat whenever I saw her.'

He left his hand on Alice's knee and it took every ounce of her will power not to hurt him.

'Mr Harrison, we didn't see you at the poker tournament this morning,' Vanessa said, as she drifted across the room and stood by the window.

Gordon had to turn away from Alice to look at Vanessa and he thankfully removed his hand. Alice took the opportunity to edge further down the couch.

'No, no, as I'm sure you know, I don't gamble, and watching other people do it is not my idea of a spectator sport.' He laughed loudly, his gaze flicking between the two ladies to see if they appreciated his humour.

Alice smiled politely but Vanessa matched his laugh with her own.

'When did you last speak with Betty?' Alice asked.

Gordon turned his attention back to her and seemed surprised at the new gap between them. 'Oh, well I saw her yesterday morning. She was coming out of the recreation building. We chatted briefly. I invited her to have coffee with me but she had another appointment.'

'How did she seem?'

'Seem? How do you mean? She seemed like Betty.'

'I mean did she seem well?'

'I suppose so,' he smoothed one of his eyebrows with his fingers. 'Why?'

Alice took a deep breath to calm herself. 'Well her death was very sudden, I guess I was just wondering if she'd been feeling ill lately.'

'Ah, well you would know better than I of course, but no she seemed well. In fact she seemed happier than I'd seen her in a while. If I didn't know any better I would have thought she'd just...you know.'

She did.

'No. What?' she asked with raised eyebrows.

Gordon's face flushed and his eyes flicked to Vanessa who was trying and failing not to look amused.

'I know, Mr Harrison. I'll explain it to Alice later.'

Alice shot her a look which called her a spoilsport, and Vanessa returned it with one that may or may not have told her to stop torturing the old man.

'Well anyway, she looked very happy.'

Alice decided to change tack. 'Gordon, have you met the new woman Nanci?'

'Nanci Katz? Yes, wonderful woman. I've invited her to dinner, and I think we've got it booked in for one day next week,' he replied excitedly.

Poor woman, Alice thought.

'Had you ever seen her and Betty together?'

'What? Not that I recall, why?'

Alice waved her hand casually. 'No reason. I haven't had a chance to talk to her yet and I just wondered how social she was.'

'Oh right. I can't say, although she was very friendly towards me, and I do remember seeing her talking to Teresa one time, and Owen too come to think of it.'

Alice frowned. For a newcomer, Nanci seemed to have talked to a lot of the residents. She shook her head to try and dislodge her suspicious nature. There's nothing odd about being friendly and trying to fit in. Not everyone had an ulterior motive. Although there was the poker game. There was definitely something weird about that. Or maybe she was a sore loser.

She heard Vanessa clear her throat and Alice realised her thoughts had been wandering again. That had been happening a lot recently. Between that and the damned cough she'd had forever she was beginning to think that maybe she was getting old.

'So,' Vanessa began and Alice snapped back her attention to the room, 'Alice is feeling a little overwhelmed with everything from today Mr Harrison so perhaps we need to let her rest.'

Alice turned a tired looking face towards her visitor. 'Sorry, Gordon, but I am feeling a little tired.'

'Of course, my dear.'

Gordon used the arm of the couch to steady himself as he stood up. He swayed a little, then beamed down at Alice.

'Let's catch up soon, once you're over this shock.'

Alice nodded which apparently satisfied him and Vanessa escorted him to the door, closing it firmly.

'Overwhelmed! I'll have you know I once stood in a room with ten people, nine of whom wanted me dead, and walked out with their wallets, and two of their phone numbers. Overwhelmed,' she repeated disgustedly. 'I have never been that in my life.'

'Noted,' Vanessa replied. 'And one day I want to hear that story. But it worked, didn't it? He's gone.'

Alice looked at her for a moment, then nodded. 'It was quick thinking. You saved me from doing something he'd regret. However next time, can we use a different word?'

'You're the boss,' Vanessa grinned.

'Good. Now what do you know about Nanci Katz?'

'Not a lot. Management handles all the paperwork for residents, I'm just the pretty face that greets them,' she laughed.

'Could you take a peek at her records?'

'All that stuff is confidential. I'm not supposed to talk about anyone's personal information.'

'I don't need to know her weight or her bra size, just where she came from.'

'You don't need to look at her records to know that. Just google her.'

'The google can tell you stuff like that? I thought it was just medical articles and cat videos.'

'That's YouTube,' Vanessa replied.

'What the heck is a YouTube?'

'A copyrighter's worst nightmare.'

'What are you talking about?' Alice said.

'Nothing. Anyway we can just type her name in and if she's ever been tagged in anything or been in the news at all it will come up.'

Vanessa looked at Alice who stared back.

'Well? Get on with it!'

Vanessa tapped away on her phone with two thumbs, faster than Alice had ever been able to do with all her fingers.

'Okay. Luckily her name isn't that common. Here's something. A Nanci Katz used to live in Christchurch. There's an article here that... Wow.' She looked at Alice.

'What wow?'

'It says here that twenty years ago a Nanci Katz was banned from the Christchurch casino,' Vanessa read.

Alice's mind raced as she connected the dots. 'Let me guess, for cheating at poker.'

'*Allegedly* cheating at poker.'

'Ha, allegedly is just a word the police use so they won't get in trouble with judges. She was cheating, and if she's a gambler then that confirms my suspicions.'

'You think she cheated at the tournament? But she lost.'

Alice leaned forward, and placing her hands on the coffee table for support she eased herself onto her feet.

'Yes. That was the whole point.'

'You've lost me,' Vanessa said, standing.

'The point is, never con a con artist. We need to talk to Teresa.' Alice started walking to the door.

'You're not going to do or say anything stupid are you?' Vanessa asked.

'Vanessa, all my stupid days are behind me.'

'Lucky you,' Vanessa muttered. 'My day's not complete unless I've done or said something I regretted.'

Closing her front door, Alice walked to the elevator and pressed the button to summon it.

'Tell me something. You can use that google to look up anyone, am I right?'

Vanessa nodded and her cheeks turned pink.

'That's what I thought.'

'I do it for everyone, it passes the time when it gets quiet. I can't tell you the number of times I've googled myself.'

'What did you find out?' Alice asked as they stepped into the elevator.

'If even half the stuff I read was true then you are my hero.'

Alice sniffed. 'Don't believe everything you read.'

The doors opened on the ground floor and they walked into the lobby.

Alice paused on the top step.

'But it was probably true,' she winked.

NINε

Teresa wasn't at her apartment, but as they left Stumpy they ran into Les who told them he'd just seen her at the café.

When they walked in they saw her huddling with Nanci at one of the tables furthest from the door. Teresa looked strained, and then guilty when she spotted them approaching.

'Alice! We were just leaving,' Teresa said, then followed Alice's eyes to the full coffee cup on the table in front of her. 'I mean...'

'Won't you join us?' Nanci asked.

'Thank you,' Vanessa replied.

No one spoke until the two of them were seated. Alice noted that Teresa refused to look her in the eye, suddenly finding her coffee cup the most fascinating thing in the world.

'It's a great shame about your friend,' Nanci said.

'Yes. It's never easy when someone close to you passes away.' Alice studied Nanci, who in turn was studying her back.

'It makes the whole poker tournament seem a bit silly,' Teresa said.

'It was always a silly thing,' Alice retorted, then sighed when it looked like Teresa was about to burst into tears. 'I mean it was always just a bit of fun,' she continued in a softer voice.

Teresa looked at Nanci with cheeks darkened. 'Of course.'

Alice sighed again. 'Look, I don't care that you cheated, Teresa. I even respect you a little more for it. But I am curious as to whether it was your idea, or yours,' she turned to Nanci.

'Cheated!'

'It was mine,' Nanci replied calmly.

'Nanci!'

'No sense denying it, Teresa, especially in light of what happened and what Alice just said. The tournament was just a bit of fun.' She turned to Alice. 'Teresa and I were talking and she said she didn't see the point of entering this year because you were bound to win again, so I offered to help her.'

'How'd you do it?' Vanessa asked.

Nanci just stared at Alice, with an almost challenging look on her face.

'This is a complete shot in the dark, but I'd imagine she got herself assigned to my table and lost on purpose, lasting just long enough to learn how I played. Maybe found some tell that I don't know about. Then she told Teresa what it was, and I'm guessing also told her what her own tells were. Close?'

'I'm glad it wasn't a real shot in the dark, or there'd be an extra hole in my head about now,' Nanci said wryly.

'How do you possibly know all that?' Teresa demanded.

Alice inwardly enjoyed the amazed expression on her face. Being underestimated had proven extremely useful over the years.

'I imagine she used to be like me,' Nanci said.

'A gambler?' Teresa asked.

'I had quite a few jobs during my working life,' Alice admitted.

'I *am* sorry about your friend. I only spoke briefly with her but she seemed nice. And I'm sorry about the tournament. As you said, it didn't mean anything so I didn't see any harm in helping Teresa win. And it's not like I taught her to count cards or anything.'

Teresa choked on her drink and quickly hid her mouth with a tissue as she coughed.

I bet you tried.

'No, quite right, there was no harm other than to my ego. I'm glad that Teresa won, and once the shock of Betty's death has passed I'm sure her victory will make a nice distraction from everything else that happened this morning.'

'Thank you, Alice. I'm sorry my competitive nature forced me to take such drastic action. I was just tired of losing to you. I so desperately wanted to win for a change.

Alice waved her hand dismissively, then patted Teresa on the arm. 'It was very cunning and I'm proud of you.'

'So no hard feelings?' Nanci asked.

'Not at all. Although one day we will have to sit down and play another game of poker, now that we understand each other a little better.'

Alice and Vanessa left the two women to finish their drinks and walked out into the sunshine.

'Was that like looking in a mirror?' Vanessa commented as they made their way back towards the main building.

Alice snorted. 'I was a lot of things over the years, but common gambler was never one of them.'

'She beat you, so obviously she wasn't that common.'

That earned Vanessa an elbow to the ribs and she stepped away laughing. As they reached the Olympic building, Alice stopped.

'Time for a quick swim?'

'No,' she muttered. 'But what was Betty really doing here yesterday morning?'

'I can't understand you when you mumble.'

'I'm not mumbling, I'm thinking quietly with words.'

'Sure, my mistake.'

Alice opened the door to the building. Immediately inside was a small reception area with a desk that wasn't usually... *attended* or *peopled* or whatever the politically correct term for *manned* was. Alice struggled to keep up with what was and wasn't allowed anymore, but then she'd never paid that much attention to it when she was younger either.

To the right was a glass door, through which she could see the heated pool with a head and two arms visible, ploughing through the water.

Directly ahead was a wide corridor that led to the rest of the complex. Alice marched past doors leading to massage therapists, physiotherapists, changing rooms, and the large recreation room filled with games and books and a massive television.

'What are we doing?' Vanessa asked as Alice pushed open the glass door leading into the gym.

'I saw Betty come in here yesterday morning. When I asked her about it she lied and said she was seeing Peter.'

'But Peter wasn't working yesterday. Garth was.'

Alice nodded as she scanned the room. The weights might have been a little lighter, but otherwise it was just like any other gym, except there were fewer mirrors. Retired people had less desire to watch themselves in the mirror as they exercised. Stationary bikes and treadmills were lined up against one glassed wall, where users could watch people swim or, twice a week at 8am, partake in water aerobics. Her friends raved about it, but Alice couldn't see the point of dressing to come to the pool, getting into your swimsuit to work out, then dressing again to go home. It seemed more work to get to the exercise than to actually do it.

Against the opposite wall were the weight machines, and at the end were some dumbbells and other free weights. A man stood with his back to them, a weighted bar at his feet. She couldn't see the number written on the weights, but they looked heavy. He squatted down, carefully grasping the bar in his hands, then gave a little wiggle of his bottom as he set himself, before shooting upright, hauling the bar with him. Seconds later his arms were directly above his head and he held the pose for a moment before dropping the bar in front of him.

He turned and Alice's mouth dropped open in surprise. It was Les.

'Well done,' Vanessa said.

Les rubbed the side of his face, leaving a smudge. Looking at his hands Alice saw they were covered with white powder.

'I didn't know you came here, Les,' Alice said.

His face flushed, although it could have been from the exertion. He glanced towards the door and out to the pool before crossing the gym floor.

'The thing is, I don't really want Freda to find out.'

'That you're coming to the gym?' Vanessa asked.

'What I'm doing at the gym.'

'Why on earth not?' Alice said. 'I would have thought she would love the idea of her man becoming a muscle bound He-man.'

Les's cheeks darkened further. 'It's just I'm... I'd just rather she didn't know, for now.'

Alice put her hand on Vanessa's arm. 'Of course, Les. It's your secret to have, and ours to keep. Although we surely can't be the only ones that have spotted you here.'

Les shot another look towards the door. 'No, but you're the only ones who know Freda well enough to mention it to her.'

'We understand,' Alice replied. 'But tell me something. Do you come here the same time every day?'

'No, I'm usually here in the morning, but Freda was a little upset over Betty so I stayed with her this morning.'

'Two morning's ago I saw Betty come into the building at about 8am. Were you here?'

Les nodded, dislodging a strand of slicked hair, which draped across his forehead. Alice resisted an urge to reach out and push it back into place. 'I was, but I didn't see Betty. She didn't come into the gym or the pool. After lifting I sit on the bike for a while and then have a spa. It helps with my recovery. I would have seen her.'

'Which means she went into the rec room, or to the physio,' said Alice.

'Or she got a massage,' Vanessa suggested.

Alice shook her head. 'No. I tried to persuade her to go and see Georgina one time and she said she'd rather lay in a field and let sheep run over her than take her clothes off and have a stranger poke and prod her.'

Les shrugged. 'I know what she means. Sorry, I can't be of any more assistance, but I need to get back to my workout before I seize up.'

'Of course. Be careful, Les, I wouldn't want you to hurt yourself with those weights.'

'Don't worry about me,' Les smiled. 'It's all about technique, and mine's perfect.'

'What now?' Vanessa asked as they left the gym.

Alice poked her head through the door of the recreation room, but it was empty of people. The doors to the other rooms were firmly shut. 'Now I need you to try and find out if Betty had an appointment with the physio.'

'I thought you said she hated the thought of strangers touching her.'

'She hated the thought of a massage. Physio is different, it's medicinal.'

'Okay, so let's say she did have an appointment. How could that possibly be related to her death?'

Alice enjoyed the warmth of the sun on her face. The soft breeze carried a hint of freshly cut grass, which overrode the smell of chlorine from inside. 'Everything's relevant until it's not,' she said.

'That's like saying everything's hot until it's cold,' Vanessa replied.

Alice grinned. 'Nothing like that at all. Can you find out or not?'

'Of course I can. All the appointments are run through a central system. I just need to be at my desk.'

'Right, you go do that, and keep working on the list of who was at the tournament. I'll see you at my place at 5pm.'

'What are you going to do?'

'I'm going to chat with Freda before Les gets finished here. She's always more chatty when her husband isn't around.'

'Sneaky,' Vanessa said.

'Practical,' Alice replied.

'See you later, and don't forget the pizza you promised.' Vanessa walked away with the sort of walk that said *I could skip or even run if I wanted to and it wouldn't be a problem*. It had been a long time since Alice had walked like that.

A short time later she was being ushered inside by Freda. As they sat on the couch, and Alice declined the offer of tea, she thought that Freda appeared to have been crying. It made her feel guilty that she hadn't shed more tears herself for Betty.

'It's just such a tragedy,' Freda said. 'And I feel so guilty, like I was the one who killed her.'

TƐN

Alice stared at Freda, trying to get a sense of whether the woman was being literal. She looked so upset. Something was definitely going on.

'What on earth do you mean by that?' Alice asked.

Freda reached over to the coffee table and plucked a tissue from the box. She dabbed at her eyes before replying. 'I did something silly. Les has been going out a bit more than usual recently and I happened to see him one day with Betty. They were sitting on that bench by the rose garden and, oh I don't know, I assumed something was going on.'

She stopped to blow her nose.

'You confronted them,' Alice guessed.

'The thing is, Les has always been faithful, through everything over the 54 years we've been married, so I have no right to think that anything was going on. But I've started feeling a little insecure lately, and he's been secretive about something. He's started plucking his nose hairs again. It's been years since he's done that. When I saw him and

Betty talking and looking so cosy I put two and two together and got—'

'An affair.'

Freda smiled at her sadly. 'Silly, isn't it?'

Alice thought it was, but daren't say it aloud. 'So what did Les say?'

If possible Freda looked more miserable. 'I didn't confront him. I waited until he left and I said something to Betty.'

'I can imagine how well that went,' Alice replied.

'She denied it, which of course she would, but I was too angry, and I told her to stay away from Les. I stormed off and a day later she was dead. I can't help thinking what if it was my fault for some reason that she...'

Alice placed her hand on Freda's arm as she dissolved into tears.

'Unless you have some supernatural powers I'm not aware of, Betty dying had nothing to do with you. You're not a witch, are you?'

Freda laughed which turned into a cough and then back into a laugh. 'My mother-in-law did always accuse me of putting a spell on Les, but I think she was just being a bitch.' Her mouth dropped open as she looked shocked. 'I mean... I can't believe I said that.'

'Why not? She probably was.'

Freda looked around, then nodded slightly. 'Maybe a little bit. I know I was being silly, this whole being jealous thing is new to me.'

'You have nothing to be jealous about,' Alice reassured her.

'Do you know what his secret is?' Freda looked at her sharply.

'It's not my place to say anything, but I can tell you it has nothing to do with another woman.'

'Oh.'

Freda looked like she had a million follow up questions and was struggling to decide which one to ask first, so Alice quickly changed the subject.

'Freda, yesterday at the tournament, did you see Betty acting strangely just before she died?'

'Strangely? I don't understand.'

'I'm just trying to find out if she was feeling unwell beforehand or if it was sudden. I'd hate to think she wasn't herself and I missed it.'

'Yes, I see.' Freda wiped her eyes and stared into the distance, considering. 'She seemed fine to me, although I didn't pay much attention to anything other than Les's table at the start. After Teresa beat you (I still can't believe that by the way) I did spot Betty stacking some poker chips on the table. I turned around to talk to Les and that's when she must have collapsed. Such a tragedy.'

'Do you know whose chips she was tidying up?' Alice asked with a frown.

'No idea,' Freda replied, pulling a fresh tissue from the box, deftly folding and tucking it in her sleeve. 'Does it matter?'

'No, no, just an idle thought.'

They chatted for a few more minutes, then Alice left Freda looking miserable. Having concluded that her sharp advice to "Stop moping over a man" wouldn't help, Alice had wisely kept it to herself and instead departed with a less helpful: "It'll all be fine".

Her next port of call should have been to the dining room, the scene of the tournament. She wanted to check out the tables to see if she could figure out whose chair Betty died beside. However, as soon as Alice stepped into the lobby her stomach growled so loudly she was surprised the replacement concierge's head hadn't shot up from the phone or book she was engrossed in.

Deciding a snack was required before further investigation, Alice returned to the elevator. As she pressed the button she felt something soft slide past her. She looked down to see Maddy sitting there. When the cat saw Alice looking she produced her trademark meow of starvation.

'Never con a con artist,' Alice told her, earning a second more pitiful noise from the feline.

The doors slid open and Alice stepped into the elevator. She turned to see the cat still sitting there waiting.

'Oh for goodness sake, come on then.'

As if understanding her, Maddy sprang inside before the doors could shut.

'I must be losing my touch,' Alice muttered.

Maddy yowled in agreement.

The cat stuck close to Alice until they were inside her apartment, where it jumped onto the kitchen counter and sat down. Alice picked her up and moved her to one of the stools. By the time she had retrieved a can of tuna from the cupboard and turned back around, Maddy was sitting on the bench again. Alice hissed at her, receiving a yawn in return.

'Fine, but you're not eating up there. And you better have a clean butt.'

Maddy proceeded to prove it by licking herself in that exact area. Alice wanted to believe the cat could understand her, but thought coincidence was a more likely explanation.

She opened the tuna can and placed it on the floor, barely getting her hand out of the way before the cat jumped down and shoved her mouth inside.

With the sound of slurping in her ears, Alice fixed herself a sandwich and sat down to watch a game show on television. As she answered another question correctly her phone beeped. A message from Amanda. Being raised by Alice it was no wonder she'd gone into the family business, persuading other people to give her their things. She was often absent for weeks at a time, and out of contact for a lot of that, but Amanda tried to check in with her grandmother whenever she could.

As usual her text was simple: "I'm still alive. Are you?"

Alice sent back an affirmative and switched off the television, deciding she was more intelligent than the contestant on the game show. She looked at Maddy who was lying in a patch of sun.

'Time to go, cat.'

The only response was a lazy tail twitch.

'I don't blame you. It looks nice. Only trouble is I wouldn't be able to get up again.'

This time there wasn't even a twitch, just the rhythmic rise and fall of a temporarily full stomach.

'If I leave you here how do I know you won't pee on the carpet while I'm gone?'

Maddy opened one eye as if to say, please stop talking to me.

Short of bending down and picking her up, Alice had no choice but to leave the cat where she was and hope for the best.

Taking the elevator back to the lobby, she made her way into the dining room, and found that she wasn't alone.

In the middle of the room Gavin stood staring into space. When he heard the sound of the door he turned, his face devoid of emotion.

Alice shivered.

ELEVEN

Gavin blinked and seemed to see her for the first time.

'Hello, Alice. Sorry, I was somewhere else for a moment,' he said and his face relaxed into a smile.

'That's quite a stern face you've got there,' Alice replied.

He laughed, 'I was in the military, Alice. A good death stare was mandatory if you wanted to climb the ranks.'

'Yes, I imagine it came in handy. With that skill, I'm surprised you're not better at poker.'

'So am I,' Gavin admitted with a shrug. 'But it was never my thing.'

Alice stepped further into the room. All the poker chips had been cleared away and a stack of clean plates and cutlery sat on the side table ready to set the tables for the next meal.

'Are you waiting for dinner?' she asked.

He glanced at his watch. 'No, I'm going over the events of the poker tournament again. I thought it would be easier to do if I was in the room.'

'Why?' Alice came closer.

He gave her another shrug. 'Call it professional habit. During my career I was responsible for sending a lot of men into potential war zones, and every single one of them that didn't come home, I made damn sure I knew why. I realise that this place is just a halfway house while we wait to head off into the great beyond, but when someone dies unexpectedly I get an itch in the back of my brain that can only be scratched when I have answers.'

'People of your age die all the time,' Alice said.

'Your age? I hate to tell you this Alice, but we're in the same category.'

She flapped her hand dismissively. 'I passed your age a long time ago and I intend to attend all your funerals.'

'Morbid.'

'But not sinister. Not intentionally anyway.' She grinned at him. 'Do you suspect foul play?'

'Foul play? I may have been alive at the same time as Agatha Christie but the words *foul play* have never crossed my lips. Of course I don't believe anything untoward happened, I just like to know things, to have things resolved. In this case I'd like to know if poor Betty was suffering from something undiagnosed, or if it was a case of food poisoning or something else that might require us to be on guard.'

Alice nodded. She also liked to know things, and right now she wanted to know if Gavin was telling the truth. His tell in poker was quite obvious, but in life she had yet to get a sense of him.

'Have you discovered anything?' she asked.

'Everything had been cleared away by the time I got here, so there's not much to see.'

She thought he seemed put out, but then he was probably used to people not doing things without his permission.

'Do you remember who was sitting at the chair Betty was beside when she collapsed?' Alice asked.

'What? No, can't say I do, not exactly. Everyone was paying attention to your table towards the end and no one was sitting down. I think Gordon was at that table when the tournament was going but can't be completely sure.' He smiled ruefully. 'I was too busy getting my rear flank handed to me by you.'

Alice inclined her head at the compliment, then moved around the table. There was a time when she would have remembered every person that had been in the room, where they sat, what they were wearing, and probably the value of any jewellery. But the years had taken the edge off her memory, and she no longer had any interest in stealing the jewellery.

Gavin's comment had jogged something loose, but it was just out of her grasp. Alice walked over to where she had been sitting for the first round, pulled the chair out and lowered herself into it.

Slowly Alice scanned the room, trying to recall the tournament. A clear picture snapped into her mind.

Gordon had been sitting at the table, next to him had been Owen, then a woman she knew in passing, Judy or Jackie something, the dealer was a member of staff, and the fifth player...

Alice frowned, she couldn't recall who the last person was. Vanessa would be able to find out from the sign-up sheet. The important thing is that she remembered whose chips Betty had been tidying when she died.

'Everything alright, Alice?' Gavin asked.

She smiled at his concern. 'I'm fine. I guess I got tired from jogging all those memories.'

Gavin sat down opposite her. 'Have you met the new woman, Nanci?'

'I have.'

'I've only talked to her for a short time, but I find her intriguing,' Gavin said.

She's a con artist, was what Alice wanted to say, but instead she said, 'She seems an interesting character.'

'I might ask her for coffee.'

Alice struggled with the right reply. It wasn't her place to say anything, but then she didn't want to see anyone taken for a ride (unless she was the one doing the driving).

'Gather your intel first.'

'What do you mean?'

She shrugged. 'You like to know things. We don't really know anything about her. I'm just suggesting you find out a little bit more before getting involved.'

Gavin replied briskly. 'Goodness me, I'm not talking about getting involved. Just getting a coffee. But I see your point, always better to know more.'

'Are you done here?' Alice gestured around the room.

'I'm not sure what I expected to find, but it's probably preposterous to think that Betty's death was anything but her time to go.'

Alice pondered his words after he left the room. The same doubts persisted, a new one popping up every time she tried to squash one. Perhaps he was right and this whole thing was a foolish quest by a silly old woman. Alice frowned. She'd never called herself silly before. Stupid, yes, occasionally an idiot, but never silly.

Alice made her way back to her apartment and scrubbed the already clean kitchen bench. Even Maddy's presence, crawling along the carpet chasing the slowly fading patch of sunlight, wasn't enough to bring her out of the funk.

Such was her distraction that she didn't even check the security camera when there was a knock at the door.

'Pizza time yet?' Vanessa asked when Alice opened the door.

She looked at the clock on the stove and saw it was after five. 'Go ahead,' she waved at the kitchen counter where the landline sat.

Vanessa tucked her hair behind her ears. 'Already ordered it. I got you a no cheese, gluten free, vegetarian pizza.'

Alice gave her a dirty look. 'There are several words in there that should not be in the same sentence as the word pizza.'

Vanessa's grin dissolved into a laugh. 'Actually I ordered lots of meat, not so much cheese on yours, with garlic bread and potato wedges.'

Alice's eyes narrowed. 'How did you know what I normally order? We've never had pizza together before.'

'Did you forget? All deliveries have to come via the front desk.'

'Of course. Good detective skills,' Alice said. 'What else have you learned?'

Vanessa went and sat on the couch. She tapped on her tablet, then showed the screen to Alice, who sat down next to her.

'This is all the people who signed up for the tournament, and the tables they were at.' She swiped upwards on the screen and a new list of names showed up. 'And these are the people who were watching. Although I can't be sure that's all of them. I was a bit busy for some of the time.' She cast a guilty look in Alice's direction.

'Don't worry, Vanessa. This was better than I was expecting,' Alice said. Then she heard her granddaughter's voice in her head reminding her that sometimes she could come across as blunt. Actually her exact words had been, "stop being a mean old lady".

'What I mean is most young people can't see past their cell phones.'

The look on Vanessa's face suggested that wasn't much better.

'Because young people are all about me, me, me.'

'Riiiight,' Vanessa said in a disappointed tone. 'If that's the way you feel...'

Alice stifled a sigh. Things were so much easier when people didn't get so easily offended. 'Not you personally, just...'

'Just all my friends and everyone I know,' Vanessa finished.

'Yes, exactly. Now back to this list. It looks pretty complete to me, although...were there any other staff there? Apart from the ones working the tables.'

Vanessa's eyes widened. 'Only Tracey from what I can remember. Why?'

'Just being thorough.'

'You don't suspect Tracey do you? I know she can be a pain sometimes, but she's not evil. I don't think.'

'We don't even know if there's a crime, so no point in excluding suspects just yet,' Alice said.

'For the possible crime.'

'I know how it sounds.'

Vanessa shrugged. 'Tracey declined my annual leave application for next week because I didn't give her enough notice. Even though I don't think she killed anyone, I'd be happy if she was slightly dodgy.'

'Alright then. This is the table that Betty died at. She was stacking poker chips at Gordon's chair.'

'Gordon! So d'you think he was the target?'

'I think we need to find out how Betty died,' Alice said. 'Do you know what happened to her body?'

92

'It's at a funeral home in the city. They're waiting for her family to make the funeral arrangements.'

Alice leaned back against the couch and rubbed her fingers and thumb together on her left hand. It was a habit she'd picked up years ago. The rhythmic motion helped her think.

'We can't ask the family to get an autopsy because we think Betty was murdered,' Vanessa said into the silence. 'They'll never believe us, and I'll probably get fired.'

'What for?' Alice asked.

'For bringing the Silvermoon Retirement Village into disrepute.'

'Tell me the truth. Is that the first time you've used the word *disrepute*?'

'Yes, I feel so grown up.'

'We don't need the family to authorise an autopsy.'

'Ew. We're not doing it ourselves,' Vanessa said with wide eyes. 'I'm happy snooping, but draw the line at dissecting.'

'Dissecting! Betty isn't a frog in a biology class.' Vanessa's face flushed and she looked towards the window.

'Do you own a suit?'

'A suit? Like a business suit?' Vanessa asked, still facing away. 'I've got a white blouse and a jacket at home that could work. Why?'

'Because I need you to be a lawyer,' Alice said.

'What?'

Alice always enjoyed the look of surprise she could elicit on other people's faces. Vanessa's was a classic combination of confusion, puzzlement, and surprise.

'A lawyer. We're going on a field trip.'

TWELVE

'I want to go on record as saying this is a really bad idea.'

'See, you're talking like a lawyer already.'

The previous evening when Alice had outlined her plan, Vanessa had seemed excited, but standing outside the McDonald and Hope Funeral Home, she was having second through to a hundred thoughts.

'They'll never believe I'm a lawyer,' Vanessa argued. 'I'm not smart enough.'

Alice gripped her arm tightly and glared at her. 'You listen to me. I never want to hear you say you're not smart again. It's that sort of thinking that will hold you back from what you really want to do in life. Self-belief is the most important tool in any woman's arsenal.'

'Tool belt.'

'Eh?'

Vanessa smiled. 'You don't have tools in arsenals, they go in tool belts.'

Alice loosened her grip and smoothed the fabric on Vanessa's sleeve. 'And you say you're not smart. You don't have to be a lawyer, you just have to look like a lawyer.'

Which she did, in a short black skirt, white blouse, and a black jacket. Her hair was swept back in a pony-tail and Alice thought it was a good thing Vanessa hadn't managed to find some glasses on a string. It was a fine line between lawyer and librarian.

Alice had borrowed some clothes from Teresa, supposedly to try them for size before she bought her own. Teresa had impeccable taste in clothing, and although she had a bit more meat on her bones than Alice, the grey dress and jacket, accompanied by a silk scarf and diamond brooch that Alice had acquired during her working days, meant that she looked the part of grieving friend.

The building they entered was on the edge of Wellington city, an old concrete structure backing onto the railway lines, and beyond that the large sports stadium. A smartly decorated reception was painted in muted colours and furnished with soft chairs on one side, and a desk on the other. A subtle bell rang as they walked through the door, and a woman in a pale green uniform popped out of the door behind the desk.

'Goodness me, please take a seat,' the woman said when she saw Alice.

Alice stifled her irritation. Everywhere she went these days people treated her like she was about to take her last breath just because she looked old, when she'd rather make the most of being alive to keep on moving.

'Thank you, dear,' she said in a frail voice, allowing herself to be guided by the arm to one of the soft chairs.

'May I get you something? Tea? Coffee?' the woman asked. She appeared to be in her late forties, and the name tag on her uniform declared to the world that her name was Beatrice.

'Nothing for me, thank you,' Alice replied with a smile.

'If you'd like to wait here I'll get one of our sales managers to come and talk over our package options with you,' Beatrice said.

'My client is not here for her own funeral arrangements,' Vanessa began. 'She has a more delicate matter to discuss with a manager.'

'Your client?'

'Viola is my lawyer,' Alice informed her. 'She is a bit officious, but she is, on this occasion, correct. I would like to speak with your manager about something.'

'Of course. I'll see if Mr Watford is free.' She hurried to the desk and picked up the phone.

'Well done, Vanessa,' Alice murmured.

'I think I'm going to throw up.'

'Later, dear.'

'Mr Watford will be out in a moment,' Beatrice relayed to them from across the room.

As if waiting for the introduction, a door opened and a young man walked through. He wore the same uniform as Beatrice, and his name tag read "Greg Watford, Assistant Manager".

'Good morning. Would you come this way please,' he said in a deep voice full of assurance.

He led them through the door, down a short corridor, and into a small room with four chairs and a coffee table. He gestured to the chairs, and closed the glass door behind them.

'How may I help you?' Greg asked once he'd taken his seat, addressing his question to Vanessa.

This could be easier than I hoped, Alice thought. 'Two days ago a woman was brought here from the Silvermoon Retirement Village,' Alice began.

Greg held up his hand. 'I'm sorry, it's against company policy to discuss the deceased.'

'A wonderful policy, which gives me a great deal of comfort should I find myself in your care after...' She studied his face without appearing to, so she could gauge his reaction. Sure enough his eyes narrowed slightly and he straightened his tie.

'Of course.'

'The thing is, it's...this woman, Betty, there is a possibility that she might be my long lost sister.'

'Oh?'

'Yes, it's a complicated family history that I won't get into. However I need to be sure as I'm...'

She waited to see if Vanessa would jump in as planned.

'My client is wealthy and she has no other family, and she is 97 years old and suffering from terminal liver failure.'

'Why don't you tell him all my secrets,' Alice grumbled loudly.

'You're the one who wanted to come here,' Vanessa reminded her.

Alice glanced at her in time to see the eye role Vanessa gave Greg, who grinned at her.

'As it stands Mrs Harper has two choices for her vast estate. Leave it to her cat, Mr Wigglesmith, or find the sister she last saw 70 years ago. We uncovered some information that suggested Betty might be her sister and we went to the retirement village yesterday, where they told us the bad news.'

'That's terrible,' Greg said. Alice watched him not so subtly checking out Vanessa's legs.

'Exactly.'

'I understand that Betty has children, and if she turns out to have been my sister I want to make sure they get some money. But I'm not giving it away to strangers. I need to be sure she's my spaghetti,' said Alice.

'Your what?' Greg asked.

'Betty spaghetti,' Alice said in a tone that suggested her own eye roll.

'Ah, I see. What I don't see is how I can help.'

'I realise that she would have changed a lot over the decades, but I'm sure I would recognise her if I saw her.'

'I'm afraid that's not possible,' Greg replied with a frown.

'Technically it's possible, just not permitted,' Vanessa chimed in.

'Well, there's the wishes of the family,' Greg began.

'Of which, my client is saying she might be one. Tell me, will it be an open casket funeral?'

'That hasn't been arranged yet, we're waiting for the deceased's daughter to fly in tomorrow.'

'However, if it was an open casket then the body would be visible to anyone, correct?'

'Well, yes but—'

'So all we're really asking for is a preview,' Vanessa said.

'But we are still preparing the deceased,' Greg protested.

'Betty,' Alice wailed, covering her face in a dainty handkerchief she pulled from the sleeve of her jacket.

'It's just...'

Vanessa put her arm around Alice and shot Greg a disapproving look. Then, to completely shatter his defences, she reached up with her other hand, pulled her hair free from the ponytail and ran her hand through it.

'I suppose a short, off the books, viewing would be alright,' Greg said in a weak voice. 'I'll just go and set things up, if you will please wait here for a minute.'

As soon as he closed the door Alice uncovered her face to reveal a smile.

'The hair thing was a nice touch, although a bit premature,' she said. 'He was about to cave anyway.'

'Sorry,' Vanessa answered with a blush. 'I got caught up in the moment and to be honest, I've always wanted to try that with a man.'

'You never have before?'

'It always seemed so corny.'

'It is, but also highly effective. I used it when I was your age. Nice to know men haven't changed that much,' Alice said with a soft laugh, before adopting a solemn look.

A split second later Greg opened the door. 'This way ladies.'

He led them through the door opposite the meeting room, down another short corridor and into a small windowless room. It was empty except for a table in the middle covered in a body shaped white cloth.

Alice walked over to the table and folded the cloth down, revealing Betty's face. She heard Vanessa gasp, and felt a twinge of sadness at seeing her friend's still, pale face.

She felt Vanessa step up next to her.

'What are we looking for again?' she whispered.

Alice wasn't quite sure. Any signs of foul play seemed a bit general, even if she knew what those signs were. She already knew there was something odd about Betty's fingernails.

Alice wished she'd done some of that googling thing, or at least got Vanessa to do it.

'Is it...' Greg asked.

'I think so. It's been a long time but...' Alice paused and leaned in closer to study Betty's face. She shuffled sideways a little to block Greg's view, then reached out a hand and gently pried open one of Betty's eyes. The pupil stared unresponsively at the ceiling and told Alice absolutely nothing except to confirm that Betty was dead. Something that had undoubtedly already been confirmed by several more qualified people.

As she was straightening up Alice noticed several tiny sticks lying on the table in the space behind Betty's neck. They looked like stray white hairs but the way they lay it seemed like they were stiff, like they were covered in hairspray.

'Oh dear,' Alice said in a wavering voice. She pulled her handkerchief out again on the pretext of wiping her eyes. As Vanessa put an arm around her shoulders Alice scooped up the hairs with the handkerchief, before turning to face Greg.

'It's not my sister. I was so hoping it was her, but this poor unfortunate lady is a stranger.'

'I am sorry to hear that,' Greg replied. 'Let me show you out.'

The way he hustled them out of the building it was obvious Greg was relieved to avoid the complications associated with a long lost relative.

Before he closed the front door he did make a final attempt at a charm offensive on Vanessa, who responded by retying her hair into a ponytail and turning her back on him.

'I feel a little bad at being rude,' she said after he'd closed the door. 'But he was being a sleezy pig.'

'Then don't feel bad.'

They started the slow walk back to the car.

'How do you do it?' Vanessa asked.

'What's that?'

'The way they treated you, like you were a child that needed their help. It would drive me crazy.'

Alice slipped her arm through Vanessa's and leaned on her a little as they walked.

'I'm sorry, are you alright?'

Alice grinned and straightened up.

'Bugger, I just did the same thing,' Vanessa said

'To be honest it does irritate me. I guess that's one of the reasons I don't like leaving the village anymore. I might still be the oldest there, but at least they're all less than a half century younger than me.'

'You've got way more patience than I have.'

'Of course I do,' Alice replied as they reached the car. 'But I've had more practice at it.'

'So did we learn anything? Apart from the fact that I don't like looking at corpses, especially ones I know.'

'Let's hope you don't have to see too many then,' Alice said.

Vanessa indicated and pulled out into traffic. She made a noise like she wanted to say something but cut herself off.

'Out with it.'

Vanessa glanced across at Alice in the passenger seat. 'It's just, I don't know much about what you used to do, and I wondered if...'

Alice filled in the blanks. 'Not too many but seeing dead bodies was occasionally an occupational hazard.'

Vanessa nodded.

'What exactly do you think I did for a living?'

'Exactly? I don't know,' Vanessa admitted. 'But presumably something that wasn't always legal. I mean you called yourself a con artist but what does that actually mean?'

Alice looked out the window at a city vastly different to the one she grew up in. She still had vivid memories of this place during the Second World War when she'd been young and full of confidence and together with her best friend Violet they had taken their destiny into their own hands with some morally questionable, but extremely fun, choices.

But they weren't all happy memories from back then, and suddenly Alice felt tired, not just her body, but her mind as well. She slumped in the seat and stared at nothing.

'Did I say something wrong?'

Stop this melancholy you silly woman, Alice thought. 'No you didn't. Sorry, just thinking about something. We don't have time to go over the full job description of what I was, but when this is all over I promise we'll sit down and I'll teach you everything I know.'

'Teach? I just wanted to know what it was like, not to become you.'

Alice looked at her. 'Are you sure?'

'Of course,' Vanessa replied in a tone that wasn't quite convincing. 'My parents would kill me if I turned to a life of crime.'

Alice snorted at her use of the cliché.

'Back to my original question. Did we learn anything from that?'

'I'm not sure. Maybe. There's these strange things I found by her neck.'

Alice carefully unfolded the handkerchief and stared at the thin white hairs. She reached out her fingers to pick one up and accidentally stabbed herself with it.

'Damn!' she said as she tried to extract the object with her other hand.

It was only once she'd successfully removed it that she realised she had lost the feeling in her finger. She waggled it and it seemed to work fine, but when she tapped it on the window her brain didn't register any sensation.

'Damn,' she repeated.

'What happened?' Vanessa asked.

'I think I may have just poisoned myself.'

THIRTEEN

'Well I don't know what you stuck yourself with, but the effects seem to have worn off and all your blood tests came back normal.'

'That's not good enough,' Vanessa told the ER doctor. 'Do you mean to tell me you can't find what caused this? That's ridiculous, what sort of doctor are you?'

'A busy one. However I can assure you that we have ruled out any immediate danger, and if Mrs Atkinson still refuses to stay the night...?'

Alice nodded. Staying a night in the hospital was a slippery slope at her age. It starts with one night, then suddenly it's two, and eventually you never leave.

'Then there is nothing more we can do at the moment. Your blood pressure is a little low, but that's not unexpected at your age. Do you have someone at home that can look after you?'

'I can take care of myself,' Alice said firmly.

'I'll make sure she's alright,' Vanessa replied.

'Right, then I'll arrange the discharge papers.'

'Before you go, any idea what the little white hair things are?'

The doctor shook his head. 'No idea, although they look organic to me.'

'Organic?' Alice asked.

'Plant. You could try asking at a garden shop. Palmers garden shop in Miramar, the staff there might know. Someone will be in shortly with your discharge papers. '

The doctor left the room, sliding the curtain closed behind him.

'See, I told you I was alright,' Alice said.

Vanessa stared with a look of disbelief. 'You were the one who said you'd been poisoned.'

'I said I *might* have poisoned myself.'

'You said the word poison, that's all I heard. After Betty, what did you think I was going to do? Drive you back home and give you a cup of tea?'

'That's what you can do right now. I'm fine. I can feel my finger again, and you heard the doctor, I'm in no immediate danger.'

'That doesn't mean there isn't something nasty working its way through your body right now.'

Alice shuffled to the edge of the bed and slid her feet to the floor. 'I'm closing in on a hundred, dear. It'd be a miracle if there wasn't something nasty working its way through my body. Now, let's get the piece of paper from the cute doctor and go ask someone about these hairs that aren't hairs.'

Vanessa threw her hands up in disgust. 'You're so...'

'Stubborn? Frustrating? Annoying? Yes.'

Before Vanessa could argue further the curtain slid open and a nurse handed them the discharge papers.

'Take it easy for a few days, Mrs Atkinson, and if any further symptoms appear then please come back in.'

They thanked her and the nurse hustled out of the room, followed by the women at a more sedate pace.

'I'm taking you home,' Vanessa said.

'Yes, dear. Right after we go to Palmers.'

'No, I'm taking you home now. Then I'll go to Palmers by myself.'

Alice considered continuing the argument, but the truth was she was tired, and Vanessa could easily find out the information without her.

'Okay.'

Vanessa frowned at her with suspicion, then nodded and marched towards the car, only to come back after a few paces to offer her arm to Alice.

'You know, you make it hard to exit triumph-antly,' she muttered.

'Yes, dear.'

'Stop it,' Vanessa grumbled.

So Alice did, remaining quiet the rest of the way home, and not even objecting when Vanessa insisted on accompanying her up to her apart-ment, although she drew the line at the suggestion of a Dora.

Alice felt that a cup of tea was in order, but decided to just sit on the couch for a few minutes.

She was woken by a loud thumping on the door. Alice checked the door camera to see Vanessa standing outside, and went to open it just as Vanessa's arm was stretched backwards ready to bang on the wood panel again.

'Why did it take you so long? I was about to break the door down. Or at least go get the override code from reception.'

'You only knocked twice, you know how long it takes me to get to the door,' Alice replied, stepping aside to let Vanessa enter.

'I was knocking for five minutes!'

'Oh. Well what did you forget?'

'Nothing, Alice. I've been to Palmers. I've been gone for almost two hours.'

Alice looked at her watch, confirming Vanessa's story.

'I must have drifted off.'

Vanessa's face went pale. 'Can you not use that term? Especially after what I found out.'

'Tell me all about it while I make us a cup of tea.'

Vanessa perched on one of the kitchen stools while Alice put the kettle on to boil and pulled cups and teaspoons from the cupboard.

'It turns out that what you found are spines from the Ongaonga plant. It's a stinging nettle found all over New Zealand.'

'Really? Then why did my finger go numb?'

'Because it's a highly poisonous plant.'

Alice paused what she was doing and stared at Vanessa.

'Deadly?'

'The person I spoke to had to do some research as they don't normally sell deadly plants, but they said not usually. There are some reports that people have died from being stung.'

Vanessa tapped on her phone, then slid it across the countertop to Alice. It was a picture of a long thin green leaf edged by sharp white needle like hairs.

'What are the symptoms?' she asked.

'It can be quite painful, and cause the area to go numb.'

Alice rubbed her finger. 'So why did it kill Betty and not me?'

'I don't know for sure, but according to the research I did one of the side effects from getting stung is a drop in blood pressure. Didn't the doctor say your blood pressure was low?'

'He did, but it's always been a little on the low side.'

'Maybe the effects aren't as severe the second time around. If these had already poked Betty then maybe she got the worst of the toxin. Did she have low blood pressure?'

Alice looked at Vanessa.

'You want me to look at her records, don't you? Are you trying to get me fired?'

Alice laughed. 'No, I'd miss you too much. Besides I know she had low blood pressure. She had to take pills for it every day. Used to drive her crazy, she hated having to remember taking them. She had one of those pill containers with the days

110

of the week on them, but she would say to me that it only worked if she could remember what day of the week it was.'

Vanessa took off her jacket and let her hair loose from her ponytail. She caught Alice watching her.

'I actually prefer it loose,' she smiled. 'Only sometimes it gets in the way. So was Betty confused about the days of the week on Wednesday?'

'Not in the way you're implying.' Alice snorted. 'She was a farmer all her life, weekdays and weekends didn't mean much on the farm. The cows still needed to be milked on a Sunday.'

'Oh.'

Alice finished making the tea and handed Vanessa hers. She blew the steam away from her cup, then set it down on the counter.

'I never saw the point of blowing on drinks. Like your breath is magically going to cool the tea enough so you don't burn your lip on the boiling water,' Vanessa said.

'It does seem a bit silly.'

'It's like when people give you food and tell you it's hot, and you take a bite anyway and they look at you like you're a little crazy for not listening to them and...'

'What?'

Vanessa sighed and drummed her fingers on the counter. 'I'm trying not to consider what this all means, because there were no stinging nettles in the room when Betty died. In fact there are none on the property, at least none I've ever seen, which means her getting spiked wasn't an accident, which means that someone killed her, which is crazy because who would want to kill Betty? And if someone did kill her then that means…'

'That someone we know killed her,' Alice finished. She looked at the miserable expression on Vanessa' face. If you want to forget all this and go back to work—'

'What! Of course not. It's just. Shouldn't we tell the police?'

-'Tell them what?' Alice asked. 'That we think our friend was poisoned by a leaf by someone unknown for some reason unknown?'

'Okay, so not the police. Why don't we ask Tracey's niece? She just became a detective and we could talk to her off the record.'

'I don't think there is such a thing, despite what television would have you believe.'

'Please?'

Alice shrugged. 'If you think it would help then sure, go ahead.'

Vanessa looked at her watch, then gave Alice a rueful smile.

'You already called her didn't you?' Alice said.

'She'll be here in five minutes.'

'Should I be annoyed or impressed?'

'Hopefully more impressed than annoyed.'

'We'll see. But Vanessa, whether or not the police take this seriously, I'm not going to stop until I find out who killed my friend. And when I do they better pray that the police get there before me.'

FOURTEEN

'It's pretty thin,' Judith said.

Alice shot a *told you so* look at Vanessa who seemed to be deliberately avoiding her gaze.

'Like wafer thin,' Judith continued. She was wearing a grey suit, and had made a point of telling them she was squeezing them in during a break in her work day.

They'd explained what they'd learned, and what they suspected, and it was going about as well as Alice had expected.

'You were the one who thought it might be suspicious earlier,' Alice reminded her.

Judith held up a hand. 'Actually I asked the question and was reassured by my aunt that it was unlikely to be suspicious.'

'And now we're telling you differently,' Vanessa said.

'No, what you're telling me is a bunch of ideas loosely connected by one giant leap.' Judith's expression softened as she looked at Alice. 'Look, I get it. You've just lost a friend. It's hard, but that doesn't mean this was anything but natural causes.

She was in her eighties with low blood pressure and who knows what else wrong with her. And to be honest, from what my aunt has said, no one had a motive to kill Betty.'

'You checked!' Vanessa said in triumph.

'No,' Judith replied gently. 'I simply asked Aunt Tracey what sort of person Betty was. It was a polite conversation. She was upset by the death.'

'Well, we won't take up any more of your valuable time, detective,' Alice said getting to her feet.

'But—'

'Will we, Vanessa?'

Vanessa shut her mouth and glared in response.

Judith paused at the door. 'And I don't want to hear about either of you harassing residents with your theories, understood?'

'Of course, detective,' Alice replied.

They waited until the elevator doors closed on Judith before shutting Alice's front door.

'We're going to harass some residents with our theories, aren't we?' Vanessa asked.

'Of course. She didn't tell us not to.'

'She just did,' said Vanessa as they walked back to the couch.

'No, she said she didn't want to hear about it. So we make sure she doesn't hear about it,' Alice replied.

They stared at each other for a moment then laughed, which for Alice rapidly turned into a coughing fit.

'Stop it,' she said to Vanessa when she had herself under control.

'Stop what?'

'Looking at me like I'm going to expire any second. It was just a cough.'

'Sorry, can't help caring,' Vanessa told her.

'And I appreciate it, but this is going to get tiresome very quickly if you call for a stretcher every time I sneeze. I promise to tell you if I'm not feeling well. Good enough?'

'Depends. Do you mean it?' Vanessa asked, tucking her hair behind her ears.

'You're catching on.'

'You're worse than my grandmother.'

'Thank you.'

'It wasn't a... Never mind. Alright, so the police aren't interested. What now?' Vanessa asked.

'Now we think we know *how*, so the next questions are *who* and *why*?'

'According to all the shows on Netflix it's either to do with money or sex and I don't think it was...' Vanessa stopped, her face red.

'It's alright Vanessa, you can say it. Betty didn't have much of one and even less of the other.'

'I didn't mean...'

'Yes you did, and that's fine, because you're mostly right. Mostly. But just to spare your poor cheeks from turning permanently into beetroots, let's look at the possibility that money was the motive. Betty was comfortable, but not rich, as far as I know. Although she was pretty taciturn when it came to money, so she might have been loaded. I think we need to take a look around her apartment.'

Vanessa sighed. 'Why not? I've seen her dead body twice. Breaking into her apartment doesn't seem like much of a violation.'

'Excellent attitude. Although, as you can legally obtain the key and she's dead, it's not technically breaking in,' Alice said.

'Do you want me to call Judith back here and you can try that theory with her?'

'Just go get the key and I'll meet you at Betty's.'

When Alice opened the front door, Maddy, who had been sitting next to the elevator, stretched and walked slowly into Alice's apartment.

'How did she get up here?' Vanessa asked.

Alice shrugged. 'That's our next mystery.' She watched the cat stroll over to the patch of sun by the window and flop down. 'Now that's retirement,' she mumbled, closing the door behind her.

In the lobby they split up, Vanessa heading behind the reception desk and through the door to the back offices, while Alice exited through the front door. She spotted Owen walking towards the rose garden and followed him.

When Alice had first moved into the complex and heard there was a rose garden, she'd had visions of a couple of rose bushes tucked away in a corner. While it *was* tucked away beside the Olympic complex, that was about the only thing she had been right about. Surrounded by a waist-high hedge, the rose garden was home to dozens of rose bushes of different colours, sizes and (according to the small signs planted in front of each bush) species. Alice had made the mistake of saying out loud that she hadn't realised there were multiple species of roses and had spent the next hour being lectured by Freda, the resident anthophile. She'd had to ask someone what that word meant and had decided it fit Freda exactly.

In the middle of the rose garden were two wooden benches, back to back, both with small brass plaques advising who had donated them. Alice had heard that it was a tranquil place to sit, surrounded by colour and quiet, but stopping to smell the roses was never a saying she'd had much use for.

Alice entered the garden through the gap in the hedge and saw Owen standing before a bright yellow rose bush. As she approached he reached out and broke off a flower.

'I'm pretty sure they don't like you doing that,' Alice said.

Owen turned with a sad smile. 'The roses?'

'They probably don't like it either, but I was talking about management.'

He stared at the flower in his hand, then shrugged. 'Unless they're keeping a tally I don't think they're going to miss one.'

'Do you mind if we sit?' Alice asked. 'I've been doing far too much walking today and my legs are reminding my hips that they never liked exercise much.'

They settled themselves onto one of the benches, the sun warming Alice's back. She had to admit it was peaceful. The concrete and glass structure of the recreational building loomed over the tops of the rose bushes, and to their left past the edge of the small hedge was a bigger hedge that guaranteed the residents privacy from their neighbours and the rest of the world.

'Owen, I think it's time you tell me about Betty and the money,' Alice said firmly.

Owen raised his eyes from the rose and looked at her with a troubled expression. 'There's the matter of confidence.'

'Betty is dead. And I'm not convinced it was by natural causes.'

She'd been going for a gentle push, but by the look of shock and disbelief on his face, Alice had achieved that with all the subtlety of a freight train.

'What on earth are you talking about?'

She quickly told him what she and Vanessa had discovered. By the end the shock had worn off but disbelief was still firmly in place.

'You can't possibly think someone killed Betty. I'm sorry but that is just..'

'Preposterous? Ludicrous? Outrageous?' The corner of Owen's mouth twitched. 'I've gone through all the *ous* words Owen, but there's no way that she got stung by Ongaonga nettles naturally.'

'But why would anyone want Betty dead?'

'Which brings us back to Betty's secret. It could be a motive.'

Owen nodded slowly. 'I see. Well I guess telling you can't hurt now. It *was* to do with money, in a manner of speaking, as you guessed earlier. I wasn't really helping her myself, it was never my area of expertise, and it had been a long time since I'd worked directly with customers, so I just provided her with one of my old contacts.'

'In the bank.'

'Yes, at the bank.'

'Contacts for what?' Alice asked, finding it increasingly difficult to stifle her impatience.

'Gold. Buying and selling, specifically.'

'Gold,' she repeated.

'Yes, you know, that yellow stuff, worth a bit,' Own replied with another twitch of his mouth.

'Yes, I've heard of it. What *specifically* did Betty want help with? Buying or selling?'

'Selling. She had recently come into a quantity of gold and wanted to know how to sell it. Banks don't really handle that sort of thing, it's usually done through gold dealers, but a man I had worked with had some experience in that area so I gave her his name and number.'

Alice sat back in her seat and considered the implications. 'So why did you want to talk to me about it? It seems a straightforward thing.'

Owen nodded. 'The transaction wasn't the problem. I was just hoping that you could persuade Betty to put the gold into the safe in the main office here.'

'She had the gold with her! In her apartment?'

'Yes. She told me she'd had a lifetime of fighting with banks and other institutions and that she didn't have the strength to do it now so she was keeping the gold with her.'

'Where did it come from?'

'She didn't tell me. She just said that it arrived recently, and she was grumbling about how much the courier cost.'

The skin on the back of Alice's neck prickled and she rubbed it with her hand. 'How much gold are we talking about?'

'I'm not sure exactly. Roughly about ten kilograms, I think?'

'Ten kilograms?'

'Yes, roughly.'

'Unless roughly means you're nine and a half kilos out, that's a lot of gold. What's that worth?'

'It depends on the day's price of course.'

'Roughly,' Alice said, earning a proper smile.

'Roughly... I would say about half a million dollars.'

'Bloody hell.'

'Yes.'

'No, you silly boy. Bloody hell, you've just described the perfect motive for murder.'

'Oh...' Owen responded as her words sunk in.

'And bloody hell, where is it now?'

FIFTEEN

Considering she out-aged him by at least a decade, Alice should have been struggling to keep up with Owen as they hurried to Betty's apartment, but it was Owen who was puffing to catch up.

'You were walking two strides to every one of mine, how did you beat me?' Owen said, wheezing as they reached the big front doors.

'Because you're old and slow and I'm just old.'

When they approached Betty's front door, Vanessa was leaning against the wall, tapping on her phone. She looked up as they got closer and Alice immediately saw that something was wrong.

'I don't want to talk about it,' Vanessa said, shoving her phone into her pants pocket.

'Talk about what?' Alice asked.

'About…. Oh. Nice try. Hi, Owen.'

'Good morning, Vanessa.'

Vanessa looked at Alice.

'I told him our suspicions and he informed me of something interesting. Let's talk about it inside.'

Vanessa unlocked Betty's front door using her key and pushed it open, stepping aside to let Alice go in first.

The room didn't look like they did on crime shows, with furniture torn apart, pictures smashed and lamps overturned, but Alice could see that someone had definitely searched the apartment. Betty hadn't been a neat freak, but she wasn't a slob. Cupboard doors were ajar, the coffee table had been dragged to an odd angle as if someone had moved it so they could look under the couch.

A quick check in the bedroom revealed similar disturbances. The wardrobe doors were wide open and several shoe boxes had been pulled out and opened.

'What's wrong?' Owen asked.

'Someone's searched the place,' she replied.

'I was here yesterday and it wasn't like this,' Vanessa said. 'Tracey asked me to check the apartment was secure and I popped my head in. That coffee table was definitely straight and the kitchen cupboards were closed. What were they looking for?'

'At a guess, about ten kilos of gold.'

'That's a hell of specific guess.'

'It seems our mild-mannered Betty was a gold tycoon,' Alice told Vanessa. 'Recently anyway.'

Vanessa looked thoughtful. 'That's a hell of a motive for murder,' she said, looking around the room. 'What would ten kilos of gold look like?'

Owen shrugged. 'It depends on its form. It could be in bars or coins or nuggets....'

'Or one big piece?' Vanessa asked.

'Well,' Owen scratched his cheek and adjusted his tie, 'the largest nugget ever found weighed 78 kilograms, so it's not unheard of.' He saw Alice's expression. 'I was curious when Betty told me about the gold so I did some research. Anyway that was found in Australia. The heaviest nugget ever found here was only three kilos. I'd be surprised if it was all in one piece.'

'Could it be flat?' Vanessa looked over at the bookcase. 'Like in a book?'

'A very big book perhaps,' Owen conceded.

Alice had visited Betty several times, but had never paid close attention to the titles on display, assuming they were romances or the cosy mystery books most people her age read. She was basing this on the two women she'd seen in the dining room reading books with topless men on the cover.

When Alice stepped closer to inspect the bookcase, she was surprised to see that Betty preferred the horror genre (unless romance had changed considerably over the years). All of the titles on Betty's shelf included either *blood*, *death*, or *vampire* (and in one case all three).

'That's unexpected,' Vanessa said as she pulled one of the books off the shelf. '*Too Many Vampires*, mmm the movie was better.'

'I guess you never really know someone until they're dead,' Alice replied.

'Don't tell me you have books like this,' said Vanessa as she replaced the book.

'I prefer stories that make you think rather than blink.'

Vanessa smiled. 'I like that. I'm going to use it.'

'Be my guest,' Alice muttered as she ran a finger along the tops of the books. There didn't seem to be any missing and none felt different to her touch, like their pages might be glued together. She checked the other shelves but they all appeared unremarkable as well.

'I'm not sure I feel comfortable with this,' Owen said. 'We shouldn't really be going through Betty's things.'

Alice turned to face him. 'Then wait outside, because we need to figure out if the murderer got what they came for and the only way to do that is to search for it.'

The troubled expression on his face increased.

'Owen,' Alice said with a sigh. 'You knew Betty, as well as anyone did. She was very pragmatic so do you honestly think she would mind us doing this?'

Owen took his time replying before finally nodding. 'I suppose she wouldn't. What can I do to help?'

'You search out here. Vanessa and I will take the bedroom. Call out if you find anything.'

With Vanessa doing all the heavy lifting, it took them 30 minutes to search the entire apartment. There was no sign of the gold. Vanessa even checked the freezer, although Alice advised that it was traditionally diamonds that were hidden in the ice tray. And just to be certain the gold wasn't hidden in a tub of cookie dough ice cream, Alice tasted several spoonfuls.

Alice stood in the middle of the lounge, while Owen straightened the couch cushions and Vanessa nudged the coffee table back into place.

'They must have taken it,' Owen said.

'It looks that way,' Vanessa replied.

Alice wasn't convinced. She had more faith in her friend's sneakiness. The question was, if it wasn't hidden here, then where was it.

She turned to Owen. 'You said you told Betty that she should put it in the office safe. Do we know that she didn't? Vanessa?'

Vanessa shook her head. 'She would have asked Tracey.'

'Can you find out?'

'I could say I need to do a complete inventory of Betty's belongings before her children get here and did she have anything in the safe.'

'Good. Off you go. We'll regroup at my place at dinner time and compare notes.'

'What are you going to do?' Vanessa asked.

'We have the motive, now I need a suspect. It has to be someone who was in the room during the tournament. With all the residents and staff, I think there were thirty names on the list.'

'You suspect the staff?'

'The only people I don't suspect, apart from me, are you and Owen,' Alice told her.

'But I know the staff.'

'Do you? Or do you just chat to them at work?' Alice said. 'How well do you actually know them?'

She could tell she was making Vanessa uncomfortable, but now that she was sure it was murder, and why, Alice was more determined than ever to get revenge for Betty's murder. *Justice*, she corrected herself.

'I'm not particularly happy with the idea that it was one of the residents either,' Alice said. 'These are people we see every day and though they are many things (liars, thieves, boring, I never pegged any of them as killers.'

'Right, well let's hope it's one of the residents.' Vanessa's face took on a panicked look as she realised what she'd said. 'I mean—'

'It's alright, dear, we know what you meant, don't we, Owen?'

Owen nodded.

Vanessa left looking more troubled than ever.

'That girl seems more upset now that the murderer could be someone she works with than the very idea that there was a murder in the first place,' Owen remarked.

Alice looked around Betty's apartment one last time, trying to identify the nagging feeling she had that there was something she was overlooking.

She nodded absently. 'No one likes to think that their colleagues are capable of killing. It could make staff morning teas quite awkward.'

They closed the door and Alice checked that it had automatically locked behind them. She thought about installing one of her old tricks so that she would be able to see if the door was opened again, but decided against it. For one thing she didn't have a match, and secondly it looked like the apartment had already been searched so it was unlikely the person would come back. Unless there was more than one person after Betty's gold, but that thought made her head ache. Briefly she wondered if she was up for all this investigating business. Her legs hurt, her head hurt. She was exhausted.

'If I'm hurting I'm breathing,' she murmured to herself.

'What's that?' Owen asked.

She flapped her hand to indicate it was nothing. What she needed was to talk to her granddaughter.

'I'll catch up with you later, Owen,' she said as they stopped outside Stumpy. The sun sat low in the sky casting long shadows over the lawn. 'In the meantime don't talk about this with anyone.'

'Don't worry. It's not the sort of thing that casually comes up in conversation.'

She nodded grimly. 'We don't know who did this and until we do, assume everyone is out to kill you.'

'What?!'

'I'm kidding. But let's just say someone has already killed for the gold. If they hear you talking about it they might assume you know more than you do. Best to keep quiet.'

She left Owen wearing a troubled expression. It seemed she was dispensing fear everywhere she went today.

As she walked past the café she glanced in and happened to see Nanci sitting at a table by herself.

Alice changed direction and stepped through the open door.

'The usual, Alice?' Connor asked from behind the counter.

'Takeaway, please,' She pointed at the table where Nanci was sitting.

'Alice, join me,' Nanci said with a wave at the seat opposite her. She waited until Alice was settled in her seat before asking, 'How are you holding up?'

'Oh, it's never easy to lose a friend, is it?' Nanci shook her head. 'Lord knows I've lost enough people close to me over the years. It always gets to you.'

Alice hesitated then decided to press ahead. 'Nanci, I think you and I are similar, at least in our previous working lives.' She paused to watch Nanci's response.

'I'm flattered that you think we're in the same league,' Nanci replied.

'So you know who I am,' Alice said with narrowed eyes.

Nanci sipped her coffee. 'Let's just say if you're who I'm pretty sure you are then you were the gold standard in our business.'

Alice snorted dismissively, but couldn't help inwardly flinching at the mention of gold.

'My reason for talking to you is twofold,' she said, 'although perhaps they're the one and the same. Teresa is my friend, and she can be a pain in the behind, but I'd hate to see her get taken in. If she is part of your long game then it's best you stop now.'

'I'm retired,' Nanci said.

'So am I,' Alice replied. They both waited to see who would twitch first.

Nanci sighed. 'Alright,' she said. 'Teresa is a fool and I could easily take her for everything she's got. But I really am retired. This is where I'm planning to live out the rest of my hopefully long life. I'm not going to mess that up. That thing with the poker tournament was a favour. For a new friend. That and I wanted to see if you were as good as I'd heard.'

Alice decided to accept her words at face value, or at least give the woman that impression. Her tea was delivered to the table and Alice stood up.

'Just out of curiosity, what would you have done if I *was* up to something?' Nanci asked.

'You've done your research on me?'

Nanci nodded.

'London 1969.'

Nanci's face paled. It was a satisfying response.

SIXTEEN

Alice read the list of names again. It was pointless trying to strike anyone off it, because every time she did a nagging doubt surfaced and she immediately put the name back on again. The trouble was that none of them struck her as a cold-blooded killer. Or a warm-blooded killer for that matter.

The only two people she could cross off the list with any certainty were herself and Vanessa. In theory she should also remove Owen as a suspect because he was in love with Betty and because he'd told her about the gold, but then love was also a powerful motive.

Moodily she watched Maddy, who was lying on the other end of the couch. As if sensing she was under scrutiny the cat opened one eye.

'Who did it?' Alice asked her.

'Rowl,' Maddy replied.

'Are you sure?'

'Mraw.'

'That's not helpful. Now if this thing could translate cat,' she waved her phone.

Maddy closed her eye again and Alice went into the kitchen in search of inspiration. A couple of sips from one of her many hidden flasks later and she had no more answers but was feeling calmer.

There was a soft knock at the door and the camera revealed Vanessa standing outside with several containers of food.

'I thought pizza two nights in a row would be bad for my figure,' she said when Alice let her in.

'What on earth are you talking about? You're gorgeous.'

'Well thanks, but I'm not going to stay that way if I stress eat and pizza is my stress-eating go-to. Even now I'm craving a chicken and bacon pizza with camembert.'

Alice unpacked the food onto the kitchen bench, opening the first container to find noodles and vegetables.

'What do you have to be stressed about? Well, apart from the whole murder thing.'

'I don't want to talk about it,' Vanessa replied as she rummaged in the top drawer and pulled out two forks.

Alice took one of the forks and began loading wontons onto a plate. 'What did Ben do?'

Vanessa gave her a sharp look. 'Who said he did anything?'

'Because most of the time when people don't want to talk about something, it relates to what a man has done. Or hasn't done but was supposed to do.'

Vanessa chewed a piece of broccoli while Alice waited patiently for her to decide how much she want to reveal.

'It's Ben,' she said finally. 'He texted me to say he wasn't sure about our relationship.'

'Dump him,' Alice replied firmly.

'Alice!'

'Do you love him?'

'I really like him and we've been going out for a while,' Vanessa said.

'Right so you don't love him, and he obviously doesn't love you or else he'd say something to your face instead of over text. So I repeat, dump him.'

'But—'

'You are a confident, beautiful young woman and if he doesn't realise what he has then dump him faster than I dumped the Beverley Diamond Ring in '68.'

Vanessa tilted her head to the side.

'Very quickly.'

'You're right, I know. I do like him though.'

'Does he challenge you?'

The head tilt was back. 'I don't understand. To a duel?'

'No, fool girl, does he challenge you to be a better person? Does he try and be your knight in shining armour or does he push you to be better?'

Vanessa answered by forking noodles into her mouth, leaving a tiny trace of sauce on her lip which she wiped with a napkin before speaking. 'I guess... he tries to make everything better.'

Alice waved her hand. 'Then dump him. You deserve someone that makes you better, not safe.'

Vanessa frowned. Then there was a slow nod and Alice wasn't sure whether her message had got through. She hoped it had.

'I've got something for you,' Vanessa said through a mouthful of food. She dug a slip of paper out of her back pocket.

When Alice opened it she saw there was a telephone number written on it along with the name Zoe.

'Betty's daughter. I thought the best way to find out about the gold might be to ask a relative.'

Alice nodded approvingly and fetched her phone from the coffee table.

Dialling the number, it connected after one ring. 'Zoe speaking,' came a strong voice down the line.

Alice fumbled with the phone and put the call on speaker.

'Zoe, this is Alice Atkinson speaking. I was a friend of your mother's at Silvermoon.'

'Yes, Mrs Atkinson. She mentioned you several times. Thank you for calling.'

'I'm sorry for your loss, dear.'

'Thank you. I don't mean to be rude, but I'm just about to head to the airport.'

'I was at your mother's apartment today to water the plants and I'm afraid it looks like someone has been in there without permission.'

'Oh hell. Was anything missing?' Zoe asked in a resigned tone.

'It's hard to tell. It doesn't look like it, but I could be wrong.' Alice paused, wondering how to proceed. 'There is one other thing...'

'Yes?'

'Betty mentioned before she died that she had a quantity of gold in her apartment.'

There was silence on the other end of the phone line.

'We can't seem to locate it,' Alice finished.

More silence, then finally Zoe asked, 'How much gold?'

'I think roughly ten kilograms.'

Still more silence, then a swear word that had both Alice and Vanessa nodding in appreciation.

'She bloody told me it was a family heirloom,' Zoe muttered.

'The gold was?' Vanessa asked.

'Who's that?'

'Sorry, Zoe. My name is Vanessa, I work at Silvermoon and I knew your mother too. I was supervising Alice while she was in Betty's apartment. Management rules.'

Alice was impressed and made a circle with her finger and her thumb and held it up to Vanessa.

'Oh, I see. Well I didn't know it was gold. There was an old locked wooden box that had been in the family for decades. Longer probably. I think it originally belonged to Mum's grandfather. Mum asked me to send it to her because we're selling the farm.'

'Do you think she knew what was in it?' Vanessa asked.

'I'm not sure. I don't think so, otherwise she wouldn't have been happy for it to go via courier.'

Alice felt her mouth open slightly at the thought of a half million dollars bouncing around in the back of a courier van.

'And now you say you can't find it?' Zoe asked.

'How big was the box?' Alice said.

'Uh, a bit bigger than a loaf of bread, I suppose. The proper big loaves, not those little gluten-free things.'

Alice had never seen or eaten anything gluten-free in her life, and wasn't even sure what it meant, but she assumed a gluten-free loaf was smaller than a normal loaf.

'I should report this to the police,' Zoe sighed again.

Vanessa nodded to Alice who shook her head. 'You absolutely should, although I think it might be better to wait until you get here. It might just be that we overlooked it and I wouldn't want to waste police time,' Alice said.

'I suppose so. I'll be there first thing in the morning. Could you meet me at Mum's apartment at 9am?'

'Of course,' Alice replied.

'Thank you. I'll see you then.' There was a click followed by silence.

'Why didn't you tell her Betty was murdered?' Vanessa asked.

Alice refilled her plate with more noodles. 'Is that really the sort of thing that should be done over the phone?'

Vanessa hid her embarrassment behind a forkful of rice.

'Anyway, we've got until tomorrow morning to try and solve the murder and find the gold. Zoe doesn't strike me as someone who will let the police dismiss our suspicions.'

'Which is a good thing, right?'

'It's messy.' Alice sighed. 'Worst case scenario they ignore her and she kicks up a fuss around the village, panicking the murderer who takes off, probably with the gold. Best case scenario the police believe her and cause a fuss around the village causing the murderer to take off, probably with the gold.'

Vanessa paused, her fork half-raised towards her mouth. 'Either way we're screwed.'

'Not quite. Like I said, there's a third option: we solve the case and find the murderer before Zoe turns up here in the morning.'

'And how do you propose doing that in...' Vanessa glanced at the oven clock behind Alice, 'the next fifteen hours?'

'By spending the first part of it eating and thinking,' Alice replied, crunching on a wonton.

SEVENTEEN

It took the rest of dinner and several sips from the hip flask usually hidden in the container marked flour before Alice formed an inkling of a plan.

'Why hide the hip flasks?' Vanessa asked, disrupting her thoughts. 'You're the only one who lives here.'

Alice grinned. 'Two reasons. One, it's an old habit that I don't have the desire to break. I always hid valuable things around the house and I like to stay in practice.'

'And the second reason?'

Alice's smile grew wider. 'Because I like the thought that when I finally stop breathing, the person who goes through this place will find a seemingly endless supply of hip flasks in the most unusual of places.'

Vanessa cracked up laughing and that's when the inkling turned into a half-plan.

'Did we check the freezer? That's a good place to hide things, although it's best for diamonds. What?' she said, realising Vanessa had stopped laughing and was looking at her strangely.

'We've already had this conversation,' Vanessa said.

Alice frowned, then remembered they had talked about it in Betty's apartment.

'Right,' she waved her hand in irritation. 'I'm allowed to forget things occasionally without being accused of senility.'

'I didn't accuse you of anything.'

'You were thinking it,' Alice shot back.

'All I said was we've already had that conversation. And if you're going to get grumpy every time I look at you then I can just leave now.'

They glared at each other and it was Alice who blinked first.

'Fair enough,' she said. 'I'll try to keep the grumpiness to a minimum.'

Vanessa nodded, 'Thanks. And I'll try and avoid looking at you.

'We're beginning to sound like an old married couple.'

'Who are you calling old, grandma?'

'You've got too much sass. Why don't you go to the gym and work it out?'

Alice stopped.

'What?' Vanessa asked.

'Maybe I am losing it.'

She got up and started walking towards the door.

'Where're you going?'

'To the Olympic complex. I saw Betty go in there on Tuesday and she was carrying a bag.'

Vanessa caught up with her at the door. 'You didn't tell me that.'

'I just remembered. If she wasn't going to the gym, then why did she have a bag?'

Vanessa pushed the elevator call button. 'Because she was hiding the gold.'

'Right.'

'Why was she hiding it? Why not just leave it in her apartment.'

Alice pondered that all the way to the ground floor until they stepped through the front door and paused on the top step. Freda and Les were walking hand in hand towards the rose garden. Freda must have talked to him.

A thought suddenly came to her. 'Because she told someone about the gold,' Alice said. 'And then Betty didn't feel it was safe in the apartment, so she decided to hide it.'

They began walking towards the recreation building.

'But... the only person she told was Owen,' Vanessa said in a low voice. 'Are you saying...'

'I'm not saying anything,' Alice replied. She refused to believe her friend was responsible for murder.

'Besides,' she continued, having thought of something. 'He was the one who told me about the gold. Why would he do that if he was the one who killed Betty for it? It would have been smarter to keep quiet and look for it once he'd got her out of the picture.'

'Good point,' Vanessa said, relief evident in her voice. 'Although the cynical voice in my head says that maybe he just needed you to get him into her apartment.'

'Never listen to the cynical voice,' Alice replied. She wished she could believe her own words, but a lifetime of lying to other people had left her with the ingrained assumption that everyone else was doing the same.

As they got to the front door of the recreation centre Alice looked towards the café. Teresa and Nanci were standing outside talking. As she watched, Nanci walked away and Teresa headed in her direction.

'I've got a better idea,' Alice muttered. 'Teresa!' she greeted her.

'Hello, Alice, Vanessa,' Teresa said with a wary smile. 'What are you two up to?'

Alice looked around as if to make sure no one was listening, then leaned in closer. 'Teresa, I think you should be careful of Nanci. I don't trust her. I wouldn't want you to be taken in.'

Teresa squeezed Alice's arm. 'Don't worry, Alice. You're a dear to be concerned, but I know all about Nanci's background. I had my lawyer do some digging before I agreed to let her teach me card tricks.' She laughed at the surprise on Alice's face. 'I know I come across as a bit, shall we say, *frivolous* sometimes, but I have no intention of giving my money away. You don't know how painful it is handing over my poker losses each week. If someone shows up and decides they want to be my best friend I always get them checked out.'

'Just how rich are you?' Alice asked bluntly.

Teresa winked. 'Let's just say that I can see rich when I look in my rear-view mirror.'

Alice only just managed to conceal her irritation. If she'd known the woman was that wealthy she would have raised the stakes in poker a long time ago.

'Speaking of rich, did you know that Betty had left a considerable sum of money when she died?' She did her best to ignore Vanessa's look of shock, while focussing on Teresa's expression.

'Really?'

'Yes,' Alice confirmed with a nod, 'a valuable heirloom.'

'Oh really?'

Alice watched her closely. There was no sign of greed, only curiosity.

'Yes, a family heirloom. Betty told us she left it in the games room in a special hiding spot. Vanessa and I are going to check it's safe and hand it over to Betty's daughter at 9am when she arrives.'

'Why not put it in the office safe?' Teresa frowned.

'Well the thing is...' Alice stopped. She hadn't actually thought this far through.

'The thing is,' interjected Vanessa, 'there's no room in the safe right now, and we're going to make sure the object is secure where it is. It's just as safe where it is, especially since no one knows it's there.'

'Right,' Alice said shooting Vanessa a look of appreciation. 'Don't tell anyone, Teresa, understand?'

'Of course. Lips sealed and all that.'

'Thank you. Now we'd best press on. Remember, not a soul.'

'Absolutely. If there's one thing I know how not to talk about it's money.'

Teresa walked away towards her building while the others walked inside.

'Why did you tell her?'

'What's Teresa's reputation in the village?' Alice said.

'She's tight with money,' Vanessa replied.

'And?'

'She's loose with gossip,' Vanessa finished with a grin.

'I guarantee you she's heading for the dining room right now to not tell everyone she can find about Betty's heirloom.'

'So how does that help us?'

They walked down the hallway to the games room, and Alice pushed open the door.

'How does a flood of people coming to search for the gold help us find it?' Vanessa asked again, as they stepped into the room.

'I think most people will treat Teresa's story as nothing more than a curiosity. As far as we know there are only two people that know there's really any gold. Owen, and the murderer.'

'And you're hoping that the murderer will come and try and find it.'

'Exactly.'

Vanessa looked at her suspiciously. 'And we'll jump out at them and shout *Gotcha*?'

'Exactly,' Alice repeated.

'Got to say, I hate this plan.'

'You don't have to stay,'

'Oh sure, I'll just leave an old woman by herself to wait for a murderer. Mum will love hearing that when I go around for Sunday dinner. "What did you do this week, darling?" "Oh I let one of the residents get herself killed while I went home and ate rocky road ice cream and watched Netflix."'

'Are you finished?'

Vanessa's eyes narrowed, then she shrugged. 'Sure.'

'You know you get quite testy when you're mad.'

'Then stop making me mad,' Vanessa shot back.

'Why? It's entertaining. Now that the issue of you staying is settled, let's look for the gold.'

The communal room was about the size of Betty's entire apartment. At one end was a pool table and table tennis table, while the other end had several tables for card and board games. A full-length built-in cupboard ran along one wall, and large windows let in plenty of natural light.

There were limited places to hide a box of gold and once they'd searched behind all the books and inside all the game boxes they reluctantly concluded it wasn't there.

'Now what?' Vanessa asked.

Alice surveyed the room trying to identify anywhere they might have missed. 'The plan doesn't change. The gold might not be here, but the murderer doesn't know that, so we wait.'

'And what if someone comes in to play a game of pool?'

'It's Thursday night. Everyone is either glued to that cooking show on Channel One, or the rugby match. No one will be coming here,' Alice said.

They chose seats which allowed them to see the door clearly, but meant anyone would have to step right into the room to see them. To pass the time Alice showed Vanessa some more card tricks, then beat her six poker hands in a row. Slowly the room grew dark as the sun disappeared behind the hill.Vanessa switched on the overhead lights.

'This is a waste of time,' she said as she shuffled the cards.

'It wouldn't be if we were playing for money.'

'That's not what I—'

The door swung open.

EIGHTEEN

'Oh,' said Nanci. 'I wasn't expecting anyone to be in here at this time.' She had stepped confidently into the room and had frozen on seeing the two women.

'No? Then what are you doing here?' Alice asked.

Nanci's eyes darted around. 'I just came to play some solitaire,' she said fixing on the deck of cards.

'I'm sure a woman of your life experience would have some cards in her apartment,' Alice said in a deliberately casual tone.

'Yes,' Nanci nodded, her eyes still roaming the room. 'Of course I do, but sometimes I like a change of environment.'

'Oh absolutely.' Alice nodded.

'What are you two doing in here?'

Alice looked at Vanessa who was sitting rigidly in her seat, her knuckles white as she gripped the edge of the table. She patted Vanessa's arm.

'You haven't just talked to Teresa, I suppose,' Alice said, ignoring Nanci's question.

Nanci's eyes rested on Alice's face. She licked her lips.

'Teresa?'

'Yes, and of course she didn't tell you about Betty's missing heirloom and how it might be hidden in this room.'

Nanci seemed to be struggling with how to respond, then her body relaxed. She nodded. 'Alright, yes. Old habits and all that. I thought it might be worth a sniff.'

'To give it to Betty's family?' Vanessa suggested. Nanci smiled, then looked at Alice. 'Remember when we were that naïve?'

Alice shook her head. 'I never was. Anyway we're settling in for a long game of cards, we might be here late into the night, or even early morning.'

'Perhaps I could...'

'No, you couldn't,' Alice replied firmly.

Nanci sighed. 'Oh well, easy come easy go. Enjoy your game.'

After Nanci left the room, Vanessa turned to Alice. 'What are you doing? She could have been the killer!'

'No,' Alice shook her head. 'She's a con artist and shady as all hell, and she might have conned Betty out of the gold, but she wouldn't have killed her for it.'

'How can you possibly know that?' Vanessa demanded, her eyes flicking to the closed door as if expecting Nanci to pop back through any second waving a killer plant.

'Because she's me. A slightly younger less polished version of me. And I wouldn't kill anyone.'

'That's lame.'

'Are you dead? No? Then trust me, it's not her,' Alice replied.

They settled down again but Alice quickly realised Vanessa's heart was no longer in the game. She looked at the big clock on the wall with its exaggeratedly large numbers and saw it was edging towards nine o'clock. Outside darkness had reduced the world to shades of black with glimpses of streetlights through the trees that lined the edge of the property.

'I'm getting thirsty. Would you be a dear and go and fetch one of the hip flasks from my apartment?'

'But what if... what if someone comes while I'm gone?'

Alice looked at the clock again. 'You won't be long, and I'm sure if anyone shows up before you get back I can stall until the cavalry arrives.'

Vanessa looked unconvinced so Alice pressed on. 'I've got my phone. I'll call you and you can come running. It'll be good for you to get some fresh air because we're likely to be here all night and I don't need you falling asleep on me.'

'Okay, but I'll be right back,' Vanessa said. She paused at the doorway and looked back, as if about to change her mind, then disappeared into the hallway and the door slowly shut.

Alice got up from her chair and searched the room again. The gold had to be somewhere and this was the only place it could be.

A little later she slumped back into the chair, tired and still without the gold. She looked back at the clock and saw that Vanessa had been gone for almost ten minutes. She felt her eyes slide shut and yawned. It had been a long time since she'd attempted to stay up all night and she was beginning to think she might have overestimated her ability to do so.

She closed her eyes once more. Vanessa would be back in a few minutes. It wouldn't hurt to rest until then.

NINETEEN

She dreamed that the door opened and someone entered the room. The person towered over her chair.

With a start she realised she wasn't dreaming. Her eyes snapped open and blinked a few times, adjusting to the light.

'Shame. I was hoping you'd stay asleep, it would have made this a lot easier.'

'Sorry to complicate your murder plot,' Alice replied. Her eyes darted to the clock. She'd been asleep for almost thirty minutes. Where was Vanessa?

'Your friend won't be coming to help. She's been detained.'

'What did you do to her, Gordon?' Alice snapped. 'If you've killed her I'll—'

'You'll what?' Gordon smirked. 'Overpower me and race to her rescue?' He gave a short laugh that sent a chill down her back.

'No, I'll do this.'

Gordon obviously felt that his superior size and the fact that he was a man meant an ordinary woman like Alice would be intimidated by his presence. He didn't consider three important factors. One, he had killed one of her close friends. Two, he might have harmed a girl she was very fond of. And three, she had never been an ordinary woman. As such, Gordon was completely unprepared when Alice's hand shot out, grabbed one of his fingers and wrenched it sideways.

There was a loud snap, and an even louder scream.

Staggering out of her chair, Alice hobbled to the door, silently cursing her old body for seizing up every time she sat for more than a minute.

In the dimly-lit hallway she should have turned right and headed for the entrance. Instead she turned left and slipped into the dark gym. Ducking down, she shuffled along the wall until she was sheltered by one of the machines. Every muscle and joint reminded her of her age.

Alice heard a door opening and held her breath, then let it out slowly when she realised it must have been Gordon going into the hallway. She reached for her phone to text for help, but it wasn't in her pocket. With a groan she realised it was still on the table in the games room.

'I know you're in here, Alice,' came Gordon's muffled voice. She was pleased to note the pain in his voice. 'There's no one coming to help you. I've got all night.'

He moved further down the hallway. She knew it wouldn't take him long to realise she wasn't in the pool or changing rooms and come back her way. Hopefully she would have enough time to arm herself.

In the dim light she made out the weights at the other end of the gym. Stepping out from behind the exercise machine she began to quietly cross the room. The minute she took a step forward the sensors caught her movement and the gym lights came on full.

Alice froze, then looked through the glass door into the hallway, where Gordon was smiling at her.

'Should have broken his face,' Alice muttered. Willing her legs to move she walked as quickly as she could towards the weights stacked neatly against the wall. As she reached them she heard the door open.

Reaching down she attempted to pick up a five kilogram disc. Her arms and back issued a fresh protest, so she ditched that idea and picked up a two kilo weight instead. Turning to face Gordon she gripped the weight in both hands and held it in front of her.

'What are you going to do with that?' Gordon asked. She could see a thin layer of sweat on his forehead and he was cradling his injured hand against his body.

'Do you remember the last time you asked me that?' Alice said brandishing the weight.

Gordon glanced down at his broken finger then gave her the angriest look she'd ever seen. If that look had been a physical thing it would have been a rabid dog crossed with a gorilla.

'Where's the gold?' Gordon asked.

'How do you know about that?' Alice replied.

Gordon glared. 'I overheard Betty talking to Owen about it. So I went snooping, trying to butter her up, but she wasn't having it. Told me to get out. Said I needed castrating. Then had the nerve to complain to Tracey about me.'

'So you thought you'd kill her and steal it.'

'It's alright for you,' Gordon raged, his voice bouncing off the walls. 'For all of you. I'm a retired civil servant. I had to sell everything I owned to afford this place. I needed that money or I was going to have to move. Betty didn't need it. Why shouldn't I have it?'

'Because it didn't belong to you,' Alice said. 'Didn't you learn that lesson in kindergarten?'

Gordon took a step forward and she waved the weight again. It was getting heavy.

'What gave you the idea about using the Ongaonga plant?' she asked.

Gordon edged forward. Now he was halfway across the floor. Alice's eyes darted around the room, identifying and dismissing possible options.

'I used to work for the Department of Conservation,' Gordon said. 'I knew the nettle's sting could be used to lower blood pressure. I didn't really mean to kill her. I just wanted her out of commission while I took off with the gold.'

'Why do it in a room full of people? Why not wait until you were alone?'

'I didn't know how long she was going to hold onto the gold for so I had to act fast.' He smiled grimly. 'No one was paying attention to me, so it was easy to slip up behind her and brush the spines against her neck. Her skin was so leathery from working outside all her life she barely felt it. I was worried I'd stick myself, even with my hand wrapped in a handkerchief. By the time she collapsed I was on the other side of the room, just another bystander concerned about poor Betty.'

Alice wished she had the strength to throw the weight at Gordon's head, but she doubted it would go even a quarter the way.

'So then Teresa told you about our discussion,' she said.

'Over dinner,' Gordon said. 'I'd searched Betty's place and knew it wasn't there. When Teresa said you thought an heirloom was hidden in this building I knew immediately what you must be talking about. I was on my way here when I saw Vanessa leave, so I followed her and made sure she wasn't going to come back.'

Alice felt anger bubble up and she swallowed it back down. She needed her wits sharp, not dulled with fury.

'You've overstepped, Gordon. You killed Betty, attacked Vanessa, and now you're after me? The police will figure out it's you.'

'Who cares,' Gordon replied with a shrug. 'I'll have the gold. With half a million dollars I can disappear and start again. So where is it?'

'No idea,' Alice admitted. 'I was sure Betty hid it in the games room but it isn't there.' She inched towards him.

'You're lying.'

'No, I... Owen, now!' she yelled.

Gordon whirled around and Alice took a big step forward, closing the distance between them. Gordon realised he'd been tricked and turned back as Alice swung the weight as hard as she could, connecting with the soft bit between his legs.

Gordon let out a strangled cry, his eyes bulged and he fell to the ground.

'Not quite castration, but it'll do,' Alice said as she dropped the weight and stepped over him.

She hustled to the door. She heard her name being shouted, as the door in front of her burst open and Owen strode in with Tracey right behind him.

'Alice, are you alright?' he asked.

'Absolutely fine,' she lied, ignoring the pain in her chest and the burning in her lungs.

'Alice!' Gordon yelled from the gym.

Owen looked over her shoulder. 'He sounds in pain,' he commented dryly.

'I hope so,' Alice replied.

'What on earth is going on?' Tracey asked, bewildered.

'Betty was murdered. Gordon did it. You'd better call the police.' Alice pushed past her and hobbled towards the door.

'Where are you going?' asked Tracey.

'To find Vanessa.'

TWENTY

'My head hurts,' Vanessa said.

'My everything hurts' Alice replied.

They were sitting in Alice's apartment with Betty's daughter Zoe, Tracey, Owen, Judith, and stretched out in a patch of sun, Maddy.

'It was very unwise,' Judith told her. 'You should have come to the police.'

'Excuse me, but we did,' Vanessa said angrily. 'You blew us off.'

Judith's face went red and she mumbled an excuse, earning another scowl from Vanessa.

'I'm glad you're alright, Vanessa,' Owen said.

'So am I. I can't believe that dickhead gave me a concussion.'

When Alice had returned to her apartment she'd found Vanessa lying on the floor, a nasty cut to the back of her head. After she came to and was seen by a paramedic, she told Alice how Gordon came to the door just as she was leaving, forced her inside and hit her with a vase from the side table.

'After you called yesterday I dug through some old family journals,' Zoe began. 'It turns out my great grandfather dug up two giant gold nuggets back when he was a gold prospector. He kept one and sold the other, which is how my family could afford the land for the farm. The remaining nugget was passed down from generation to generation until Mum decided to sell it and divide it amongst us kids so we could afford to buy our own houses.'

'That sounds like Betty,' Owen told her. 'Practicality above sentimentality.'

Zoe smiled at him. She looked exactly like a younger version of her mother.

'We still don't know where it is,' Vanessa said.

Alice struggled to her feet. She was covered in bruises and her arms and back protested. She winced as she straightened up.

'You should book in for a massage when Georgina gets back tomorrow,' Tracey told her.

'Maybe,' she replied as she slowly made her way to the kitchen. 'Wait, what?' She turned to Tracey.

'When Georgina gets back from her leave,' Tracey expanded. 'She's been on leave all week but she'll be back tomorrow.'

Alice felt the beginning of the feeling she got when she'd been stupid.

'How long has she been on leave?' she asked casually.

'For the last five days,' Tracey replied. 'Why?'

'Sometimes I want to kick my own butt, come on.'

'Where are we going,' Vanessa asked when she joined Alice at the front door.

'To get the gold.'

'Huh?...Oh. Oh!'

'Exactly.'

In a slow procession everyone followed Alice to the recreation building, where she stopped outside the massage room. She tried the door but it was locked. Vanessa leaned in and slid her card over the security reader. There was a click, and the handle turned under Alice's hand. She pushed the door open to reveal a small windowless room. Off to the left hand side was another door. A massage table sat in the middle of the room and at the far end was a small table with lots of bottles on it.

Alice stepped into the room, closely followed by Vanessa. Owen crowded into the doorway and watched as Alice stood still, her head swivelling from side to side.

There didn't seem to be many places to hide a big chunk of gold. Vanessa opened the second door but it led to a small closet, containing a rail and some empty coat hangers.

Alice's brain was working hard. She tried to think like someone who didn't have a lot of experience hiding things. It had to be somewhere easily accessible.

At the end of the room, next to the table holding all the bottles, was a large wicker basket.

A crumpled white towel was visible on top of the basket.

'Too simple,' she muttered.

She walked across the room and pulled out the towel, revealing another used towel. She pulled that out as well and found another one. The basket was half empty now. One more towel came out... revealing a wooden box. Alice reached in to pull it out, then remembered it would weigh at least ten kilos.

'Vanessa, a little help?' she gestured the girl forward.

Vanessa lifted the box out and placed it on the table. Alice fumbled with the latch, then lifted the lid, suddenly aware that the others had crowded into the room.

As gold went it was pretty unspectacular, not bright and shining like you'd expect, but dull. Yellowish. It didn't detract too much from the fact they were looking at half a million dollars.

'Whoa,' Vanessa said.

'Quite,' Alice replied.

TWENTY-ONE

'Are you sure you want to do this?' Nanci asked.

'Well, it's one way to pass the time, don't you think?' Alice replied.

They were sitting on opposite sides of the table in the dining room, a deck of cards and several neatly stacked piles of poker chips between them.

'I've already beaten you once,' Nanci reminded her.

'Well then, you have nothing to worry about.' Nanci shrugged, picked up the deck of cards and shuffled them. She dealt five cards to each of them.

'This is going to be fun,' Nanci said with a smile. Alice watched her opponent pick up the five cards and fan them out in her hand. It was small, but there was the tiniest hint of a twitch from her left eyebrow.

'Yes it is,' Alice agreed.

THE END

Author's Note

The Ongaonga plant is a real plant from New Zealand. Its spines are poisonous and there has been at least one death attributed to being stung by the plant, although it isn't usually fatal.

The largest nugget of gold found in New Zealand was 3 kilograms, but why go small when you can go big. It was important to make it worth enough money to spur someone to murder (which I know these days could be any amount at all).

Alice first appeared in Murder in Paint in a cameo and then returned in a more substantial role in Murder in Doubt. I so enjoyed writing her that I decided she needed her own series.

Acknowledgements

The business of writing a book is definitely a team effort. Although my name is on the cover, it wouldn't exist ithout the support and effort of the following:

My wonderful wife Sarah who is always encouraging and tells me off for over committing

My amazing editor Anna Golden who takes the rough edges off my words

Daniela at Stunningbookcovers.com for making the book look pretty

Emily Simmonds for being a fantastic Alpha Reader (technically it's a Beta Reader but she's much more important than that)

All the people that told me they loved the character of Alice and I better not kill her off. Well I didn't, instead I gave her a series of her own.

About the Author

 Rodney Strong quit a 9–5 job in 2016 to pursue his lifelong dream of becoming a writer (he still has the very first play he wrote at age 6). He lives in Porirua, New Zealand, with his wife, two children, and two cats.

When he's not writing he attempts to stay away from chocolate, goes for runs (sometimes), reads, and enjoys spending time with his young children (who contribute a lot to the running and craving for chocolate).

Visit his website to see more of his work and to sign up to his newsletter to receive free stories and advance news of upcoming releases.

www.rodneystrongauthor.com

Facebook: www.facebook.com/rodneystrongauthor/
Twitter: @RodneySwriter
Instagram: rodneyswriter

Made in the USA
Middletown, DE
31 January 2025